For years I've been a romance junkie, devouring each one like warm, chocolate chip cookies. Perhaps that's why I adore writing about love and passion. Passion—such a powerful word, don't you think? I'd classify myself as a late bloomer. I started college in my late forties, met the love of my life in my mid-fifties and published my first book in my early sixties. My husband and I live in Southern Virginia. We enjoy spoiling the grandchildren and traveling. My deepest desire is to write saucy, often humorous romances you'll cherish long after you've turned off the e-reader.

Santa Wore Leathers

VONNIE DAVIS

Harper*Impulse* an imprint of
HarperCollins*Publishers* Ltd
77–85 Fulham Palace Road
Hammersmith, London W6 8JB

www.harpercollins.co.uk

A Paperback Original 2014

First published in Great Britain in ebook format by Harper*Impulse* 2013

Copyright © Vonnie Davis 2014

Cover Images © Shutterstock.com

Vonnie Davis asserts the moral right to
be identified as the author of this work

A catalogue record for this book
is available from the British Library

ISBN: 9780007591787

Automatically produced by Atomik ePublisher from Easypress

To my awesome critique partners, AJ Nuest and Rachel Brimble, fabulous authors who point out when I've used the same phrase three times on the same page and remind me a participle looks nasty when it dangles. Thanks for your patience, my darlings.

Chapter 1

My new neighbor is a man-whore.
Becca Sinclair peered through the window of her townhouse, her fingertips flying over the keyboard. This new post on her "The Things Men Do" blog would definitely entertain her twelve hundred followers. Comments would amass and maybe, if she were lucky, she'd increase her audience.

Marshall, her editor at the *Clearwater Daily*, had dangled the incentive of giving her a weekly column, but only if she secured fifteen hundred followers. The poor schmuck had no idea how determined she was. Or how much women loved reading her comical, often snarky, take on the male gender.

With her desk positioned in front of the bay window in her living room, she had a great view of the goings-on in her neighborhood. This secluded vantage point had birthed many well-read posts. She raised her tiny espresso cup to her lips, inhaled its strong aroma as she sipped and read over her first paragraph on the screen.

About an hour ago, a brunette showed up at his front door carrying a box of Krispy Kremes. Just now, a blonde parked her red car behind the silver compact of woman number one. Before woman number two's stilettos hit the pavement, shirtless man-whore jogged out of his townhouse to greet her, no doubt in an attempt to head her off at the pass. Pardon the cliché, sistahs, but men ARE so clichéd, are they not?

1

Becca's gaze swept from her monitor to her neighbor and the blonde talking on the sidewalk. Man-whore must lift weights in his sleep to get a build like that. How hard would his muscles feel if she ran her hands over them? Dismissing her thought with an eye roll, she allowed her perusal to continue. Like most Floridians, he had a deep tan which, when combined with his sculptured muscles, presented a very potent male package. If she were one to notice, which she was not.

His hair was dark and straight, brushing his shoulders. When he turned, revealing his chest, there was a very nice treasure trail leading to jeans riding low on his hips. The two people moved and Becca began typing again.

The blonde gushed as she handed him a foil-covered pan. My randy neighbor peeled back the cover, swiped a finger over whatever she'd made and stuck his digit in his mouth. With the pan tucked to his muscled chest like a football, he deigned to give her a hug before she drove off.

By the time he turned and walked to his front door, he'd eaten two pastries. Evidently he's a man-whore with a huge appetite.

Becca finished her post and closed her laptop. "Einstein, are you ready for your walk?" Her German shepherd barked once in response and circled her twice. "Get your leash while I put on my shoes."

Einstein slipped his rope off the doorknob and carried it to her, his head held proudly and his backside wiggling in anticipation of their morning run. Becca tied her sneakers and did a few quick stretches before snapping the leash onto the dog's collar.

Two miles later they returned to Seashell Lane, jogging toward home in her gulf-side community on the northern fringes of Clearwater, Florida. She loved her neighborhood; a comfortable blend of retirees and small families. At least, it had been, until two weeks ago, when her new neighbor, with his constant stream of female visitors, moved in. Her gaze swept to the townhouse next to hers. The man went through women quicker than her ex-husband.

Just then his door opened, and man-whore stepped out on his small front porch. In a purely feminine reaction, she reached to smooth back her hair. Suddenly, Einstein wrenched his leash from her grip and took off.

"Einstein! Einstein, stop!" She sprinted after her errant dog.

Her neighbor pivoted. Einstein leaped, knocking him back against the door. "Whoa there, big guy!" He accepted the canine kisses and aimed dark eyes at her. "Is he yours? He's some dog." His large hands ruffled Einstein's fur. Firm biceps flexed under her neighbor's black Harley T-shirt, and the bottom of a wicked tribal tattoo peeked from beneath his right sleeve.

"Yes. I'm sorry he jumped on you. He never takes off like that." *No doubt one dog recognizes another.*

"Man, I'd love a dog like him. A man's dog, you know? I've got a cat. Not by choice, though. When my sister went off to college, she left Fluffy with me."

Man-whore aimed a wide smile at her, his perfectly straight teeth a contrast to his tan. A dimple winked. The fact he only had one dimple was the singular flaw on his flawlessly handsome face. Now that she was within five feet of him, she could clearly examine his features. Having watched him through her window from time to time, she knew he was tall and muscular. But up close, she realized he had the body of a serious weight lifter. His long, dark-brown hair was brushed straight back. The skin crinkled at the corners of espresso-colored eyes when he smiled, which he seemed to do easily and frequently. Yet, it was the vision of him holding a cat named Fluffy that nearly made her smile. *Muscle man and putty cat.*

"You live next door, don't you?" He jerked his head toward her home.

She bent to grasp the end of her dog's leash. "Yes, I do."

He extended his hand when she straightened. "Dan Wolford." His dimple flashed again and his smile did all kinds of twitchy things to her insides. "Most people simply call me Wolf."

3

I'll just bet they do.

She glanced at his hand for a second. No need to be rude, even if she didn't care for his cavalier attitude toward women. She did the polite thing. "Welcome to the neighborhood, Dan."

"Wolf, please." His large paw enveloped hers, and warmth spread upwards from her stomach, did a backflip and then dove downwards. Meanwhile, his dark gaze assessed her entire body and face, as if she were the most dazzling woman in sweaty running clothes he'd ever seen. His solitary dimple winked along with his thousand-watt smile. One dark eyebrow rose as if he were waiting for her to share her name. She wasn't sure why she hesitated. She was reluctant. Fueled by his cocksure attitude, no doubt. Now *there* was a cliché, if ever she'd heard one.

His thumb rubbed slow, lazy circles over her knuckles detonating sensual signals straight to her core. Oh, he was good at this magnetism stuff.

Wolf glanced at her prancing, panting dog. "Einstein, does your owner have a name? It looks like she's not sharing today."

Oh, for Pete's sake.

Einstein whined, his tongue lolling crooked from his mouth.

"Huh, looks like Einstein's not talking either." She tugged her hand free. "Excuse me. I have Christmas shopping planned for this afternoon. I better get going." She pivoted toward her front door.

"Have a good day, Becca Sinclair." His deep voice washed over her, sending an annoyed shiver up her spine. So the man knew her name all along and was just playing dumb. Was that sneaky arrogance or stalker-creepy?

She glared at him over her shoulder. "If you knew my name, why'd you make a big deal out of asking for it?"

He shrugged and looked down for a beat before aiming his dark eyes at her again. "When a man finds a strange woman attractive, he asks around until he finds out something about her. Mrs. Minelli, two doors down, fears you've been pining away for your ex-husband."

4

Sneaky stalker creepy.

She turned, snapped her fingers once and Einstein sat at her feet before she planted her hands on her hips. "I don't appreciate being the topic of neighborhood gossip, Dan Wolford." Her earlier blog post came to mind, but she mentally swiped it away like a nasty bug on a windshield. On her blog, he and anyone else she wrote about remained anonymous. No one knew exactly who these men were or if they even existed. No harm; no foul.

His smile slid from his face and he stepped toward her. "Mrs. Minelli also said you never smile anymore. I can see she's right. Look, I didn't mean to upset you."

She turned to leave and he reached out to grab her arm.

Einstein growled deep in his throat.

In response, Wolf's hand slipped into his pocket. "Before you go, I'm having a party tonight for my birthday. Nothing big. Family and a few guys from the station. You're more than welcome to come."

He has to be kidding. No way am I spending an evening with him, birthday party or not. "Sorry, I have plans." A pizza and a romance book. "Have a good day, Mr. Wolford." Clearly she needed to establish some boundaries with this guy. She strode the few feet to her door. Einstein followed.

"Becca, the name's Wolf," he called after her.

"Whatever," she waved her hand in dismissal, "*Mister* Wolford."

His deep, warm laughter swept over her like a balmy breeze off the Gulf of Mexico. In response, her temper whirled hot like a cyclone and her fingers curled into fists. Damn, what an arrogant man.

"Seven o'clock. No need to bring a gift. Having you there will be present enough."

Seriously? Couldn't the man come up with more original material? Was this how he spoke to every woman to coax them into his bed? And wasn't that a sad commentary on the brainpower of the female gender if even one fell for it?

"Don't hold your breath, Fluffy Daddy," she yelled as she slipped her key in the lock.

He laughed harder. "Make it seven, baby."

Seven, my ass.

Chapter 2

He shouldn't have pushed her like that. Hell, he'd be lucky if his attractive neighbor ever spoke to him again. But, wow, how dazzling she'd looked with that brimstone flashing from her hazel eyes. For some reason, the more he talked, the more they sparked. It was almost as if she were pissed at him before he even opened his mouth. But, why?

Wolf's four younger sisters had initiated him into the mystifying workings of the female mind. His naturally intuitive nature responded fairly well to their fluctuating moods. Once more his gaze shifted to Becca's front porch. Her body language had been one of total disdain and he hadn't responded well to it at all. In fact, he'd egged her on. "Yanked her chain," as April, the oldest of his four sisters, would say.

No doubt he should go next door and apologize for acting like such an ass. Maybe then he could convince the auburn-haired beauty to come to his party tonight. In the two weeks he'd lived here, she'd jogged past his window several times. Her beauty dazzled him. Her long legs were too distracting. And the tales Mrs. Minelli, an elderly neighbor, told about Becca's giving nature charmed him too. He'd never cared much for self-centered women.

He strode to her townhouse, rang the doorbell and waited.

Finally, her door opened and he was greeted with a scowl.

"What?" She tugged the lapels of her short white silky robe together.

"I…ah…" His gaze snagged on all those ample curves showcased by the slinky material. "I…ah…"

"You said that already." She fisted a hand on her hip.

Einstein cannonballed around Becca with something red clamped in his jaws. He streaked across the grass, his strong muscles propelling him as he circled both of their yards.

"Get back in here!" Becca pointed into her house.

Einstein loped across the grass and shrubbery, ignoring his owner's command.

Maybe if he acted the hero and returned the pet to its owner, he'd gain a few brownie points. "Stay here. I'll get him." Wolf took off after the dog.

Seeing he was being chased only made Einstein run faster. Wolf followed him twice around the yard in front of Becca's house. The dog leapt over a flowerbed and stopped, his head lowered, shaking his prize, his hind end elevated, wiggling in excitement.

"Give me that." Wolf stepped to the right around the flowerbed. The dog trotted to the left. In a quick move, he sprinted to the left and the dog dashed to the right. "Think you're smart, don't you?" He could have sworn the dog smiled.

Wolf leapt across the blooms, hoping to grab the smartass canine. Once he'd grabbed the collar, they rolled, and Einstein yelped. Wolf grimaced as he, too, rolled across a low-growing cactus and into the trunk of a palm tree. "Dammit."

The dog whined and dropped the fabric to lick and bite at the prickly thorns in his groin.

"Easy now, Einstein." Wolf cooed as he slipped his Swiss army knife from the front pocket of his jeans.

"What's wrong? What's going on? What are you doing with that knife?" Becca tugged on the hem of her short robe and glanced up and down the street as if she thought to run out into the yard.

"Stay where you are. He'll be fine. He's got some thorns in his hide." Wolf removed the tweezers stored in a slot in the knife and began extracting the offending needles. "We can't have an awesome fella like you in pain now, can we?" He worked as quickly as he could. "One more, big guy, and then you'll be fine." The dog licked him several times. "Yeah, I like you too. Let's keep what I'm about to do just between us, shall we?" He ran his fingers over the affected groin area, keeping his attentions on the dog's reactions. "Looks like we got them all."

"What in blue blazes are you doing to that dog? Are you performing some kind of 'beasty-wildy' on him?" Mrs. Minelli, his neighbor, punctured the air with her cane, her white eyebrows arched in question.

He fought the urge to laugh. "No, Mrs. Minelli. I was taking out thorns."

She cocked her head to the side, her cataract-clouded eyes widened. "In his penis?"

Christ! "No, ma'am. I was just helping him." He made a mental note to sterilize the tweezers later when he slipped them back into his Swiss knife.

Becca ran across the yard. "What's going on?"

He turned to tell her about the thorns and stopped. His tongue all but rolled out onto the grass. The Florida sunlight had turned her robe nearly translucent. She had legs that went to her waist, or so they seemed, except for that red patch at their juncture. Evidently her auburn hair was her natural color. His gaze traveled upward to the dusty-pink nipples showcased by the rays of sunshine. All the blood rushed from his brain to his cock. *Holy Mother of God.*

Wolf couldn't move. He couldn't tear his gaze from her. Einstein trotted to his mistress and licked her knees and, for an instant, he thought of doing the same thing. *Be cool, man.*

Becca held her robe in place with one hand and grabbed her dog's collar with her other. "How are you today, Mrs. Minelli?"

"I'm fine, but you'd better get back inside" The elderly woman pointed again with her cane. "That robe is so see-through, we can tell if your belly button is an innie or an outie."

9

Becca glanced down and gasped. "Crap!" She spun and bolted for her door, taking Einstein with her.

"I'd watch myself if I were you. She's not the kind a man diddles with. She's a decent girl." She nodded once and shuffled down the sidewalk toward her house.

Properly chastised, Wolf snatched the red lace item Einstein had dropped when he'd gotten hurt. It took a second or two of fingering it before he realized it was a thong. His gaze swept to Becca waiting on the porch. Her cheeks were nearly as red as the skimpy underwear. Most redheads' skin mottled when they blushed, but not hers. On her, the even blush was appealing.

Once he stepped onto the porch, Becca sputtered in obvious embarrassment. "I...I was about to get in the shower when the doorbell rang." Einstein leaned against her and she bent in an absent-minded gesture to pet him. Her robe gaped open and Wolf nearly swallowed his tongue at her high, firm breasts. "Thanks for getting him. He never runs off like that and he's never shown any interest in my clothes."

"Well, any male—two-legged or four—would be interested in this thong."

She scowled again.

"Look, I just came over to apologize for flirting with you earlier. I didn't mean a word of it." He hooked fingers on both sides of the red lace and all but drooled at the delicate lingerie. "You can still come to my party tonight, though."

She flinched as if she'd been slapped. Her eyes widened and then narrowed. Luscious lips formed a thin line. "I wouldn't come to your damn party if you sent me an invitation engraved on a brick of gold." She snatched her panties from his hands and slammed the door in his face.

What the hell? What did I do?

****

10

By seven o'clock, Becca had her shopping done, her house decorated for Christmas and two pans of banana nut bread in the oven. If she hadn't spent so much time at her window, catching sneak peeks at Wolf's guests ambling up the walk to his front door, she'd have been done much sooner.

The bone-thumping music vibrating through their adjoining wall announced the party was in full swing. A myriad voices, including a deep laugh she recognized as Wolf's, seeped through the stud-and-plasterboard petition. No doubt they were all having a good time.

She could be, too, if she'd accepted his invitation, but attending his soirée would imply she was another female waiting in line for induction into his harem of conquests. Cold day in hell. Only he'd have to be interested first, wouldn't he? If his earlier words were any indication, he wasn't. Which was totally fine with her. Men were a one-way street to the junction of pain and heartache.

"Becca, are you there or did you fall asleep?" Brittany's annoyed voice boomed from her cell phone. Her best friend had called to say how much she'd enjoyed today's post on Becca's blog.

"Sorry. I was watching two of Wolf's male guests pull up. Each one is more muscular than the last."

Brittany groaned in response.

"No, you can't come over. Another one just arrived. That makes a total of six guys driving Harleys."

Her best friend laughed. "Don't tell me man-whore rides a hawg, too."

"Oh, don't you know it. Big, black and noisy. Chrome out the wah-zoo. Typical show-off bike for a jerk with an overrated opinion of himself."

"Does he know you ride?"

"Don't think so." She turned away from the window. "My Kawasaki Ninja's been in the shop for over a week. I'm picking it up Monday." Her stomach growled. "Look, I'm going to hang up and order a pizza. Hope your cramps are better tomorrow."

"Me too, girlfriend." Brittany paused. "Becca?"

"Yeah?"

"I think you should reconsider and go to the party. Check out some of those good-looking guys. Maybe you could find one for each of us."

"That Midol you took musta gone to your brain, girlfriend. I am *not* going to that party. The man's an ass and I plan on staying far away from him. Night, babe."

Becca went online to order a pizza and then sprawled on the sofa with a book. At the beginning of chapter two, the oven's timer went off and she hurried to the kitchen, inhaling the aromas of nutmeg and cinnamon. She set the golden loaves on top of the stove—one for the Minellis two doors down and one for Brittany and her cramps. When her doorbell chimed, she glanced at her oven clock before hurrying into the foyer.

Einstein was at the door, barking. "Shush, now. Go get in your chair. It's just our pizza." He whined and jumped onto his recliner, crying his displeasure at not standing guard.

To her surprise, the blonde she'd seen this morning bringing a pan of goodies to man-whore stood on her small front porch. Her little black dress showcased her figure. "Hi." She was all smiles.

"Hello." What was she doing here?

"My brother-in-law sent me over. He wanted to make sure you were coming to the party." She laughed and tossed her long hair over her shoulder in a smooth, careless move. "He said he'd come get you himself, but he was afraid you'd clobber him."

"Your brother-in-law?"

"Yes. Wolf. Well, I call him Big Wolf. I'm married to Baby Wolf." She beamed another smile. "'Course my husband, Jace, gets his boxers in a twist when I call him that. Helps to keep our men off balance, don't you think?"

So the blonde was a relative, not a conquest. Interesting. Must be a close-knit family, unlike hers.

The lady extended a manicured hand. "I'm Wendy Anne, by

12

the way."

"Nice to meet you." Becca shook her hand and glanced over the woman's shoulder at the delivery guy bringing her pizza. "I wasn't planning on attending the party, as you can see."

Wendy Anne stepped aside so he could hand Becca her order. She signed the charge slip on the top of the box. "Please tell the birthday boy I wish him well and I hope he grows up soon."

Wendy Anne laughed, snatched the pizza from her and spun, keeping it out of her reach. "I'll just take this and set it out with the rest of the food at Wolf's. Meanwhile, put on the sexiest damn thing you've got and come on over." She turned and winked. "Ignore the birthday boy, as you call him. Flirt with the rest of the firemen at the party. It'll drive him nuts."

"The guys on the Harleys are firemen?"

"That's right. Wolf, my Jace and most of the men at the party are from Station Thirty-two over on Carpenter Street. Wolf heads the Marine Rescue Unit as well as serving as a fireman." Wendy Anne glanced away for a beat. "You're the first woman I've known my brother-in-law to show a real interest in since he left the SEALs." More laughter bubbled forth from this likeable woman. "He even asked me which shirt he should wear tonight. He never does that." She headed back toward Wolf's townhouse. "Get your vixen on, girl. I'm going to enjoy watching you two dance around each other. Just come on in. Door's open."

Becca closed her door and locked it. "Einstein, that whole family is nuts. 'Dance around each other,' indeed. Do you believe what she said? I'm the first he's shown any interest in?"

Einstein whined.

"Yeah. I don't believe it either. What about all the women we've seen sashaying in and out of his townhouse?" She snapped her fingers and he jumped down from his chair. "Want some kibble, baby?" He followed her into the kitchen. "Don't know what I'm going to eat."

She was not going to her neighbor's party. Although, for two

13

cents, she'd put on that slinky red dress she saved for special occasions, strut over there and retrieve her supper. Not a bad idea. She'd saunter in, make eye contact with Mr. Ex-SEAL and leave with her pizza.

Chapter 3

Wolf knew the moment Becca stepped into his living room. The hairs on the back of his neck stood on end. He swiveled slowly and the air whooshed from his lungs when he zeroed-in on her. *Holy Mother of God.*

Someone had painted a skimpy red swath of material over a small portion of her skin. It was strapless, pushing the tops of her breasts upward, inviting a man's fingers to trail over them...or his lips to taste. His fingers flexed in an unspoken command. The hem of the dress barely caressed the essentials. His gaze took a long, leisurely tour of toned thighs and calves, and his cock stood as if it wanted to get a peek at them too. Her red ankle-strap stilettos initiated fantasies of having those satiny-looking limbs wrapped around his hips while he sank into her warmth—repeatedly.

Once his gaze had slowly devoured the sight of her red toenails and snaked over every curve of her luscious body to her siren-red lips, his jeans were so damn tight his pecker would bear the zipper's imprint for days. Hell, he'd have to stop going commando if he spent more time around her.

Becca glared at him with those smoking eyes of hers, heavily made up to ensnare a man's attention—and she certainly had his. In fact, she'd captured it his first day here when he glanced out his kitchen door to see her playing with Einstein in her backyard.

With his work schedule and hers, meeting up with her to introduce himself and strike up a conversation hadn't come easy. Now that it had, he intended to get to know her better.

Their gazes connected and a current of potent awareness seemed to arc between them. Becca's eyes narrowed and she hiked her pointy chin before she sauntered toward Barclay and Quinn from the fire station. Was he seeing correctly? Holy fuck, the back of what barely passed as a dress dipped to showcase two dimples at the flare of her most excellent ass. Damn. Shouldn't that be illegal in polite society? He glared at the guys. Just what the hell were they gawking at with lust in their eyes? Freakin' perverts.

"Wow, who's the lady in red?" Cassie, his baby sister, pointed with her beer bottle. "Redheads don't usually look good in that color, but she looks fantastic. That is one killer dress."

"Yeah. What there is of it." He snatched the long neck from Cassie. "She's Becca, my next-door neighbor, and you are *not* drinking."

"I'll be twenty-one next month."

"Well, this isn't January, now, is it?"

"You're awful grumpy for being the birthday boy." Cassie frowned.

Yeah, well try being the birthday boy with a massive hard-on in a roomful of people. He brought her beer to his mouth and upended it. Lord knew, he needed something to cool off with after feasting his eyes on Becca.

Cassie looped her arm in his. "I don't need you to be my daddy anymore, big brother. You've sacrificed too much for us. All of us." She jerked her chin in Becca's direction. "You need to get a personal life. I see how you look at her. It's as if she were a pitcher of ice water and you needed a long, slow drink."

Hell, baby sister, if you only knew.

He bent to kiss Cassie's dark hair. When he'd resigned his commission with the SEALs she had been sixteen, troubled and homeless. She needed his influence and care. So had his other three sisters. His brother, Jace, newly married to Wendy Anne and finishing college, had had his own list of responsibilities. The last thing Jace needed heaped on his plate was four teenage girls crowding his apartment, taking away the privacy every man should have with his new wife. It seemed the whole family needed Wolf's help to get them through the grief of losing both parents in the hellacious fire that destroyed two homes on their block.

His CO tried talking him out of resigning and had said he had a bright future in the Navy. But as the oldest sibling, he had obligations. Family had been so important to his mom and dad. He wasn't about to dishonor their memory by turning his back on them.

"Is there any more of that fruit punch you made?" He'd like to keep her from drinking until she was legal… or thirty-five.

Cassie's eyes narrowed and she nodded.

"Why don't you get us each a glass? Lots of ice in mine." Punch was the last thing he wanted, but if it kept her away from the booze, he'd gladly suffer through.

"You are so-o-o transparent." She strode away.

"Yeah, well, you are so-o-o underage, Cassie-Bassie." He laughed when she stuck her tongue out at him.

Wolf's gaze swept to Becca. Quinn had her backed against the wall where his forearm rested above her pretty head. She was paying close attention to whatever he was saying. No doubt Quinn, the bastard, was working his charm on her. Something elemental and possessive unfurled and snarled in Wolf's gut. *Oh no. Oh, hell no!* He shouldered his way through a roomful of guests. If anyone was going to flirt with her tonight, it would damn well be him. He had seen her first, dammit.

"When is the charity bike ride for children's toys?" Becca's gaze flicked to his when he stopped next to her and Quinn.

"Saturday after next. Right, Wolf?" Quinn gave an ornery grin. "Guess who's leading the ride dressed up as Santa?" Quinn the blabbermouth jerked a thumb over his shoulder. "We voted The

17

Wolf in."

"Railroaded would be more like it. I took off work to look after Cassie when she had her wisdom teeth out, and the whole gang at the station decided to pick the least-likely candidate for the position." He sidled up to Becca and trailed a finger down her arm. "Do I look like Santa to you?"

She scowled and turned slightly out of his reach. "No, you don't. You do resemble one of his elves, though. Dopey."

"Hey," he splayed a hand over his chest. "You're breaking my heart here. Besides, wasn't Dopey a dwarf?"

She nodded and winked. "Yup, but tall or short, in your case, it fits." Pleased with herself, if her smirk was any indication, she fingered one of her dangly earrings, which was so long it kissed her bare shoulder. "Is Cassie one of your girlfriends?"

"Oh, God, no. I'm his baby sister." Cassie handed him a glass of punch. "Wolf, where are your manners? She doesn't have a drink." His sister elbowed Quinn. "Hot lips, why don't you get Becca a glass of wine. White or red?"

"I'm not staying. I just came over for—"

"She'll have white. It goes best with birthday cake." Wolf kept his gaze locked on Becca's. "Bring her a slab of cake, too, Quinn. In fact, fix her a whole plate of goodies. My sisters have outdone themselves."

"Hey, it's not every day our big brother turns thirty." Cassie took Quinn's hand and they ambled toward the dining room.

For some reason, Becca blushed a deep red. "How…how many sisters do you have?"

He sipped at the punch and set it on a nearby table. "Four. I'm the oldest, then my brother Jace." He started to point across the room, thought better of it, and stepped nearer to Becca. Placing one hand at the small of her bare back, he indicated where his brother sat with his wife on his lap. "You've already met Wendy Anne."

"Yes." She shivered slightly under his touch, which pleased him.

"They're expecting a child. They just made the announcement

18

at our family Thanksgiving meal. They lost the first baby, so Wendy Anne wanted to wait until her first trimester was over to share the news."

Becca glanced at him. "How do you feel about being an uncle?"

He laughed. "I've already bought the stroller. Rated the safest on the market. It's going to be the kid's first Christmas gift. That and a big toy wolf." He motioned with his hands. "It's got to be the size of Einstein."

"What's a baby going to do with a gigantic thing like that?"

"You just wait. The kid will drag it everywhere." He turned her slightly. "See the girl in black over by the doorway? That's April, the oldest of my sisters. She's arguing with Jenna, another sister. April's engaged and wants her best friend for her maid of honor. Jenna's feelings are hurt, but with three sisters, how can April choose just one?"

"I see her point."

With her heels, Becca was nearly as tall as his six foot two, and he liked being able to look directly into her hazel eyes. There were gold flecks in their depths. He leaned a little closer to inhale her vanilla and lilac scent.

"Is Cassie the sister who gave you Fluffy?" She glanced around. "Where is the cat?"

"Hiding out upstairs in my bedroom. She won't come down until the house is quiet again. Megan, sister number three, gave me the fur ball when she went away to University of Florida. " He slid his hand upward from the small of her back until he could wrap his arm around her shoulder. "That's her holding court with three of the firemen from our fire and rescue station. Megan's an R.N."

"You sound proud."

"I'm proud of all of them. Cassie graduated from beauty school last spring and has her own beauty shop over on Pinella. April's an engineer. Jenna works as a buyer for Macy's."

"And you're a fireman."

He smiled. "That I am, although my primary duty is to head

the Marine Rescue Unit. What about you?"

"I'm a reporter for the *Clearwater Daily*." She accepted the glass of wine Cassie handed her and sipped.

Freakin' hell. Of all the professions in the world, why that one? "A reporter? Don't tell me you're one of those lowlifes who ask victims at the most painful points of their lives how they felt when the car ran over their child or a bomb exploded in their faces." *Or when an arsonist's handiwork burned down the family's home with their parents sleeping inside.*

Becca straightened her shoulders and folded her arms at her waist. "People have a right to the news. The complete news."

"And people have a right to their privacy. Reporters are the pimple on the ass of the world."

Before his eyes, Becca morphed from a sensual, enticing breeze to a blistering tempest. "You arrogant, opinionated ass. Reporters have a job to do the same as anyone else!"

He leaned in, his temper burning hot in his gut. "Oh, and is it your job to hurt others?"

"Hur...hurt others? What the hell are you talking about?"

"Wolf." Cassie's request was barely a whisper. She wiped a tear and stormed off.

Becca stared after his sister's hurried retreat. "See, you've even upset her."

"Not me. You." He poked his finger against the bare skin of her shoulder. He took a deep breath to try and settle his raging anger and glanced away for a beat. "We lost our parents in a fire four years ago. Cassie was staying at a friend's house the night it happened."

He looked at Becca again. Her eyebrows were furrowed, as if taking in every word he uttered. "My baby sister blamed herself for not being home, felt if she had been, she might have saved Mom and Dad. Reporters hounded her relentlessly, asking her how she 'felt.'" He spat the last word. "She wasn't the only one harassed. So were the rest of my siblings, but for Cassie, combined with her blaming herself, their onslaught nearly did her in. I left the SEALs and came home to care for her and to finish raising the older three girls."

Her warm hand settled on his forearm and he welcomed the contact, reporter or not.

"I'm sorry for all your family went through. That's a horrible, horrible tragedy."

He nodded, ready to change the topic. "Are your parents living?"

"Yes. They're divorced. Dad lost his job in the weakened economy. We lost the house. Mom lost her lifestyle." She wove fingers through her long curls and sighed. "Everything fell apart."

"Yeah. Life can be a bitch."

Becca sipped her wine, her forehead furrowed. "You know, not all reporters are as aggressive as the ones your family tangled with."

He chuffed a short laugh. "Do you really want to continue down that dark path of conversation? We all have our pet peeves, our push buttons. Reporters are mine."

"So you blame all reporters for a few rogue ones with zero sensitivity? Even someone like me, who handles obituaries and the social pages?" Her hazel eyes narrowed and her lips pinched. "Golly, I bet you *really* hate the guys who cover the sports, thoughtless heathens that they are." She handed him her glass, turned and stormed out with that world-class ass twitching under her tight skirt.

He shoved a hand into the pocket of his jeans. A reporter. The first woman in years to snag his attention and she just *had* to be a freaking reporter. A soulless parasite who fed on the misfortune of others. A beautiful and enticing parasite. She stirred something in him, and he wasn't at all sure he liked it. He clunked her glass on the stand next to his. *Damn it all to hell.*

As if she were a siren and he her mindless fool, he followed.

Chapter 4

Becca fingered for her door key, hidden in the hanging fern on her porch and wiped off the dirt before sticking it in her lock. Going over to Wolf's had been a huge mistake. Huge. She'd gone to the trouble of getting made-up and squeezed into her best dress for five minutes of party and ten minutes of lecture. *Damn, what an annoying man.*

From inside, Einstein barked and whined an eager welcome.

"Becca! Becca, wait up." Hurried footfalls sounded behind her and a hand coiled around her arm. Wolf turned her to face him. "I was offensive back there. I'm sorry."

Just why did you have to make him so handsome, God? Even in the dark, his voice is deep and sensual. Couldn't you have taken some of his abundant sexiness and used it to make him more pleasant? 'Cause this guy is one rude piece of work.

She jerked her hand from his grasp. "First, you can stop putting your hands on me. Earlier today you said you were sorry for flirting with me, as if I wasn't the type of woman you found attractive."

"That's not true. I find you very attractive. What man wouldn't?"

She chose to ignore his forced compliment. After all, she'd gotten all dressed up for him and he never once told her how nice she looked. Nice? Hell, she looked hot, the big jerk. "Now you're apologizing for being impolite and insulting. Tell me, do you ever do *anything* you don't regret later?"

He backed her against the door, his dark eyes glittering in the soft light spilling onto the porch from her desk lamp near the window. Her tummy did a little twitchy thing when his thighs bumped hers. His fingers forked in her hair, angling her head so their gazes locked. "Believe me, you annoying woman, what I'm about to do next I don't plan on regretting."

His warm, soft lips covered hers with gentle sips at first as if tasting her or waiting for her to object. She would have, too, if her mind hadn't stopped working. Her whole body sparked with a sensual overload, and she trembled with its power. His fingertips massaged her scalp in miniscule circles, sending an erotic electrical current zinging down her thighs to zap the tips of her toes.

Her hands took on a life of their own and spread over his hard chest and broad shoulders. Tension rippled beneath his white, soft polo shirt as her hands explored and caressed. He tasted of beer and something sweet, whipped into a frenzy with tightly reigned male passion. Wood tones from his cologne were too appealing. Against her desires—or because of them—she pressed against the heat of his muscular frame.

He groaned her name against her lips and she was lost.

Wrapping her arms around his neck and allowing her fingers to sift through his long hair, she tangled her tongue with his. Wetness pooled and a moan escaped from the confines of her chest. How long? How long had it been since she'd felt so feminine, so aroused, so damned desperate for a man? When he angled his head to take the kiss deeper and rocked his hips against hers, the fleeting question in her mind morphed into raw need.

He took control, grabbed her bottom and rubbed her mound against his erection to increase the friction.

A rainbow of fireworks exploded behind her eyelids. Sensations staggering between pain and pleasure erupted. If she didn't end this, she'd climax on her front porch—and wouldn't that just add to his egotistical opinion of himself?

She pushed him away. "No."

His eyes were hooded and obsidian with desire. He rested his forehead against hers and took several long, deep breaths. "You're right. Not here. Not now."

"Not ever."

Caution coiled strong tentacles around her heart. She wanted this man. Perhaps that was why she watched him from her window and was so attentive to his comings and goings. Something about his bearing attracted her, and she wanted him with an intensity she'd never had with Tommy Ray. What passion they'd shared at the start of their four-year marriage soon died. No doubt a few times with Wolf and this sexual craze would fade too. Would its ending hurt as much as the conclusion of her life with her ex-husband? She wouldn't allow herself to find out. This magnetism had to cease now.

"You have a party to return to, birthday boy."

His head inclined and he feathered several kisses against her neck. She stifled a moan. It was as if he already knew her body's erogenous zones. Her nipples peaked in search of friction from his fingers or tongue.

He straightened and ran the pad of his thumb over her bottom lip. "I have to work tomorrow and the next day. We do two twenty-four-hour shifts at the station and then have two days off. My family's going Christmas-caroling at two retirement homes Wednesday evening. Would you like to come along? It's something we started on my first Christmas out of the Navy. Being with seniors reminds us of our parents and grandparents." He glanced away. "Anchors us in the season, somehow."

Pain, grief perhaps, tinged his final statement and touched her heart. "That's a very magnanimous gesture. I'm guessing yours is a family that goes all out for the holidays?" Hers hadn't since her dad walked out.

He trailed his fingertips down her cheek. "You have no idea how much we love Christmas. It tends to bring out the kid in each of us. Everyone meets at my place for cookies and hot chocolate before we head off to the nursing homes. Wendy Anne has a keyboard we take along."

"Wow. You do go all out." Would Wolf be a powerful singer or produce a flat tone? She'd love to go along just to hear him.

"The girls have already put together little presents for the senior citizens. Lotions, bath gels, stockings." He shrugged a shoulder. "Stuff like that. I throw in books. Romances for the women, books set during World War II or the Vietnam War for the men."

She hadn't expected this side of him and it surprised her. "Why would you include me in your family tradition? I'll feel as if I'm intruding."

"No. The more, the merrier. Some of the guys from the station are also going along. They bought puzzles to add to the presents we'll hand out."

"I could make cookies and candies. I love to cook, but rarely do it just for me."

"Sounds good. Come over at six on Wednesday. It'll be an early evening since the old folks tend to go to bed earlier than most." He stepped closer and took her hand in his. "Maybe we could go out for a late dinner. I'll make reservations for the two of us somewhere."

Singing Christmas carols and handing out gifts as part of a group was one thing, but dinner alone with him was more personal. She had to keep her distance. With one heated kiss, he'd melted a layer of the glacier encasing her heart. A handsome, sexy, self-assured man could do great damage. She had to deflect Wolf's allure by refusing his offer. What better way to repel him than reminding him what she was? "You'd take a lowly reporter out to dinner?"

He slipped his hands into the back pockets of his black jeans and stepped backwards. "A reporter. Yeah, I'd forgotten." He snorted a burst of laughter. "Hell, with my lips fused to yours earlier, I damn near forgot my name. I never lose control with a woman like that." His gaze shifted to the street for a few seconds, and he murmured something she couldn't distinguish. His posture and the set of his broad shoulders spoke of sadness. *Oh, girl, get a grip. Just like all men, he's a heartache with a capital H.*

"Good night, Wolf."

His dark eyes with their predatory gaze landed on her, and for an instant, they almost caressed her before emotion shuttered them. "I'm attracted to you. I won't deny it." He huffed an audible sigh and ran a hand through his hair. "I also don't like or trust reporters. Dammit, why did you have to be one?" He executed a half-hearted salute and walked away. "Good night, reporter lady."

A dose of melancholy misted her eyes and she willed the tears away. Why would she care if the man never approached her again? Or kissed her? She turned and leaned her forehead against the front door, sighing. Something about the feelings he stirred in her scared her. The man certainly knew how to hijack a kiss. For a minute he had her femininity flying high—and she feared the crash landing the ride would surely bring.

****

Salt spray moistened Wolf's face as the rubber inflatable craft sped along the causeway. He welcomed the familiar exhilaration, the adrenaline rush. Dressed in scuba gear, his gaze swept over his highly trained four-man Marine Rescue Unit as they expertly prepared for their rescue attempt. When the call came into the station from a stranded boat near Memorial Causeway Bridge, his team was underway in less than five minutes.

His diving partner, Barclay, shouted over the noise of the speeding engine, "Dispatch said the guy fell overboard?"

Wolf nodded. "Yeah. They were out here partying. Things got wild. One guy decided he could walk the boat's railing. Damn fool." He adjusted his scuba gear and double-checked his tank's gauges.

As soon as they approached the boat, passengers screamed and pointed in the direction where their drinking buddy had toppled overboard. Wolf positioned his mask and mouthpiece while Quinn steered the craft around the designated area. Dread tensed Wolf's muscles as he narrowed his eyes and scanned the area, ominously absent of anybody. Water lapped the sides of the rubber craft. He gave a thumbs-up signal to Barclay, who sat at the ready on the other side of the craft. They both flipped backwards into the water.

A sense of peace relaxed him as soon as he entered his domain. He was at home here—capable, confident and in control. Unlike when he interacted with his hot neighbor. *Fuck, man, get her out of your mind.*

Wolf swam toward Barclay and placed both index fingers side to side in the "swim together" signal and then pointed toward the left. His diving partner nodded. The water grew murkier the deeper they went. Nearly twelve minutes had passed since they'd responded to the call. How long had the man been able to stay afloat before he went under?

To his right, the water was muddier, as if recent rains had disturbed the natural order of things—or a man was struggling for his life. He tapped Barclay's arm and pointed in that direction. His diving partner nodded, and they swam toward what Wolf hoped would be their target.

Wolf spotted him hung up on something and wide-eyed with fright, his arms flailing. He approached and removed his mouthpiece, extending it to the drowning man. The victim grasped the regulator and gulped oxygen. Wolf tried calming the man with touches and hand signals, but he was beyond comprehension.

After the man had drawn several breaths of air, Wolf tried taking the mouthpiece back so he could take a breath too. In his panic, the man swung at him, increasing his grasp on the regulator and hose. If Wolf didn't get him under control, the frantic man would tear the tubing and then they'd both be up shit creek. He unbuckled the straps holding the tank to his body and slipped out of its confines. Then he wrapped the man's arms around the cylinder of pressurized oxygen.

Meanwhile, Barclay worked to loosen the man's foot from an outcropping of coral. Wolf removed his knife from its scabbard and cut the strings in the man's sneaker. For some reason, insane with terror no doubt, the man swung the tank, striking Wolf in the shoulder. For a couple of heartbeats, a blinding, searing pain made him exhale, losing what air remained in his lungs. *Foolish bastard: I've got a knife in my hand and you want to play games?*

If Wolf were a lesser man, he'd slice the asshole's foot just to give him a permanent souvenir of his stupid day of drunkenness in Florida. Barclay tapped his arm and extended his mouthpiece so Wolf could get a couple of much-needed gulps of air. He nodded his appreciation. Barclay's instinctive reaction helped him to once more concentrate on controlling his breathing, the survival technique he'd perfected in the SEALs. From his peripheral vision, the tank came at him once more and he spun away. *This guy is drunk and scared out of his fucking mind. God knows what he'll do next.*

His partner swam behind the man to prevent him from striking Wolf again. Once Wolf cut the side of the shoe, creating enough room to remove the man's foot, he slipped it free. Wolf and Barclay swam for the surface, dragging the drunk between them.

Back at the fire and rescue station, Jace handed Wolf a cup of coffee and sat across from him at the large dining table the men shared. "You seem in a foul mood today."

Wolf grunted and blew across the top of the steaming brew. His gaze swept around the living quarters the firemen and marine rescue team shared. Three sofas formed a U around a widescreen TV. Two computer desks lined one wall. Beyond them was a hallway leading to sleeping quarters and the showers. Two of his men sat on one of the sofas, playing on a Wii. Another raided the refrigerator.

Once Wolf's unit had returned to the station, he'd dried, inspected and stowed his equipment before taking a hot shower and getting dressed. Now he was trying to eke out a little quiet time before the next emergency.

"Heard your rescue was a little tense for a while."

His younger brother never did respect Wolf's need for solitude. No use in getting upset with the chatterbox. Jace was Jace, and Wolf loved the brat the way he was. He leaned back and ran a hand over his face. "Yeah. The man put up a struggle. Sometimes people fight rescuers when they're drowning. Fear overrides rational thinking. Don't know how long he'd been under by the time we got to him."

Jace narrowed his eyes. "How's your shoulder?"

"No big deal." Actually, the damn thing hurt like a sonofabitch whenever he moved it.

"Man needed an attitude adjustment. Why didn't you clock him? I heard the asshole wasn't even wearing a life preserver."

Wolf shook his head. "I'm always amazed at people's stupidity. I think the police took the whole crew into custody for a while. Hope it puts the fear of God into the tourists and sends them home with a new respect for how seriously we take water safety down here." He sipped his coffee, trying to ignore the throbbing in his shoulder. He'd sleep on a heating pad tonight, and it would be fine by morning. "How's little momma?"

Jace laughed. "She thinks she's showing already." He shrugged and reached for a handful of Christmas cookies from the holiday container one of the guys had set on the dining-room table at the station. "I'm just glad the first trimester is over. She got so depressed after the miscarriage last year. Not sure if I could handle seeing her go through that again."

"But the doctor thinks things are fine, right?" His family meant everything to him. The prospect of a niece or nephew pleased him. Uncle Wolf, the coolest uncle ever, had a lot of plans for the kid.

His brother exhaled a long, slow breath. "Yeah. Heartbeat's strong. Things are looking good." Jace's typical cocksure smile spread. "Hey, noticed you talking to your neighbor at your party last night. Noticed all the sparks flying between you two." Jace dunked a cookie in his coffee, a gawd-awful habit left over from childhood. "And I also noticed you were absent from the party

29

for a while. Did you walk her home?"

"You always did notice too much. Smartass."

Jace waggled his eyebrows and stuffed another coffee-soaked cookie into his mouth. "You interested?"

"She's a damn reporter, man." Something in Wolf's gut twisted and acid rolled.

"So?"

The kid always was dense. Wolf leaned across the table. "So, you know how I feel about reporters after the way they hounded our family."

"You need to get over that, man. Look," Jace folded his arms at the edge of the table and set his jaw in that determined way he had. "Wendy Anne's a history teacher, and you know how I've always hated history. Was I dumb enough to pass her over just because of that?"

Wolf blinked at his annoying brother twice. "What the hell does that have to do with anything?"

"If you can't figure it out, you're a bigger dumbass than I thought." Jace stood and brushed crumbs from his shirt. "Wendy Anne likes her and that's good enough for me. Reporter or not." He snatched his cup from the table and headed for the equipment room.

What did Wendy Anne's being a history teacher have to do with Becca's being a freakin' reporter? History teachers never hounded pain-filled people in the midst of mourning. No. Reporters had exclusive dibs on that callous activity. Still, none of the reporters who'd harassed his family had been Becca. No doubt she'd still been in college back then. Was it fair to lump her into the whole rotten batch?

He was strongly attracted to the beautiful Becca Sinclair. Maybe it was time to evaluate the weight of his interest in her against the weight of his resentment of reporters.

Bitterness never kept a man warm at night or heated him to distraction during the day. He drained his cup and stood, rinsing it out at the sink before adding it to a full load of dirty dishes and pressing the start button.

Laughter from the TV area drew his attention. "Wolf! Wolf, come here, you gotta read this blog." Greg motioned him over.

"Didn't know you were into reading blogs." He approached the sofa, where Greg and Quinn were huddled over a laptop.

"The wife reads it every day. She got me turned on to it. Listen to this…" Greg chuckled and wiped tears of mirth from his eyes. "'My new neighbor is a man-whore.' God, this Becca woman's got his number. Listen to her rip into him…"

Becca? He leaned across the back of the sofa to read over Greg's shoulder. *Christ Almighty, she's blogging about me.* He scanned the blog, laughing out loud at some places. She thought his sister and sister-in-law were his fuck-buddies. *Oh, darlin', have you got a lot to learn about me!*

Wolf returned to the kitchen, still shaking his head and laughing. Tonight was his night to cook for the guys. He stepped to the refrigerator and pulled out the ingredients for meatloaf. Maybe food preparation would take his mind off a certain man-shy blogger. He chopped onions and green peppers, his knife a flurry of smooth movement while he recalled thinking of her through the night, reliving the explosive kiss they'd shared. The woman was pure sensual voodoo—the magic of her hazel eyes, her silky skin and soft lips. He hardened at the memory of an aroused Becca in his arms, moaning, responding. *Dammit. Maybe she's right, I am a man-whore. At least where she's concerned.*

Wolf fisted the mixture a couple times and began shaping the two large loaves. He squeezed the contents of a bottle of ketchup over them and slid the large pan into the oven. The station's siren blared and the captain's voice boomed over the intercom with the address of the blaze, sending the firemen into a flurry of organized and automatic activity. Wolf set the timer for the oven's start and stop times before rushing to join the men in the equipment room.

Chapter 5

His two twenty-four-hour shifts behind him, Wolf stood on a ladder, hanging his second string of Christmas lights along his roofline when a rice burner droned down his street and eased to the curb in front of his section of townhouses. No one he knew drove a crotch bike, so he glanced over his shoulder and snorted. What man in his right mind would ride a hot-pink crotch rocket? When the rider tugged off the matching pink helmet, long auburn curls tumbled halfway down her back.

Becca.

Becca…on a motorcycle…in tight holy-hell-look-at-that-ass black-leather pants.

Every drop of blood in his body did a freefall to his groin. Fantasies of Becca strutted across his now-empty brain in those black over-the-knee fuck-me boots she also wore. One image had her pressing a stiletto between his pecs. The heel of his hand rubbed his chest in reaction to the sexual vision. Damn, he was lightheaded. When she leaned over, her most excellent ass toward him, as she pushed the wrinkles out of her leathers, he pivoted on the ladder to get a better look. *Holy Mother of God.*

She tucked her helmet under her arm and sashayed up the sidewalk. If she knew he was there, gaping at her, she gave no indication. He leaned out farther to gawk a little longer. How many cows had to die to cover those fine long legs of hers?

Her door opened and a canine "welcome home" barking greeted her.

"Einstein, baby, did you miss Mommy?"

The dog shot out of the door and streaked toward Wolf's ladder at ninety miles an hour.

"No! No, Einstein." She ran after him.

The ladder teetered when it took the brunt of the strong canine's weight. Wolf grasped for purchase on the top rung, but the backward momentum of the ladder had already started. He wasn't afraid of falling. As a SEAL, he'd done his fair share from aircraft, cliffs and stairways. He prepared to tuck and roll. On impact, he exhaled and relaxed to reduce injuries.

His ladder clattered to the ground beside him. Einstein dropped something and then barked as he circled Wolf. In his excitement, the dog lifted his leg against the top of the aluminum ladder. Wolf rolled to a dry spot and met a pair of black-heeled boots.

"You okay?" His sexual fantasy inquired as she stooped next to him. She was out of breath, as if she'd run.

"Yeah."

She trailed fingertips down his neck and he all but groaned in delight. "No broken bones?"

He shook his head. *Just a hard-on that hurts like hell.*

From behind her ear, she plucked a pen and poised it above a small notebook. "Tell me, Mr. Wolford, how did you feel when your arrogant ass hit the ground?" Her one finely plucked eyebrow arched in question.

He couldn't make up his mind if he was hellishly annoyed or amused. Since his cock was the only part of his body thinking right now, he'd have to let it decide. "You're enjoying this, aren't you?"

She faked a cheesy smile. "Well, you know how we reporters are. Always out for blood. Eager, well, beyond eager really, to interview people at their worst moments." Her gaze swept their side of the street and she leaned in, her get-your-sex-here perfume revving

33

his senses. "With you, I bet there are a lot of crappy moments, aren't there?"

Oh, so she wanted to play, did she? Game on. His hand snaked out and cupped the back of her neck, pulling her to him. His lips captured hers and he rolled to tuck her beneath his body. One touch of her soft lips and he was racing to dive off the cliff of sexual insanity. He wanted this woman more than his next breath. Hell, her sexual pull was more magnetic than his power to resist. He bit her lower lip and then soothed it with his tongue. A soft moan escaped her, further ensnaring him in her essence. When her hands moved across his shoulders, his slid down to her leather-encased ass and cupped a luscious curve. Damn, he couldn't get enough of her taste, of her smell, of the feel of her.

"What in H-E-double toothpicks are you two doing out here? Get a room, for heaven's sake."

Wolf released the finest pair of lips he'd ever tasted and glared over his shoulder at Mrs. Minelli before rolling off Becca. He slung an arm over his eyes and raised one knee to hide his erection. *Damn.*

"We just don't allow such lustful behavior in our development." The elderly woman pressed a wrinkled hand to her bony chest, her eyes widened in horror. "There are children in our neighborhood." Her jolly red sweatshirt read "Meet me under the mistletoe."

Becca stood and aimed an angry glare at him. "I want you to stay away from me, do you understand?" She turned to the elderly woman. "I'm sorry, Mrs. Minelli. It won't happen again."

She snapped her fingers for Einstein, who followed her inside. The door slammed behind them.

"Young man, come here." Mrs. Minelli crooked a finger as she leaned on her cane.

He rubbed his hands over his face and stood. Being chastised was the last thing he wanted. What he really needed was to sink balls-deep into one beautiful, high-handed reporter. "Yes?"

"Women need romance, not manhandling."

He shook his head. "I wasn't—"

Her cool hand, peppered with age spots, rested on his forearm. "Maybe not in your mind but, believe me, that's how she saw it. It was evident in her eyes when she looked at you. Flowers. Candlelight and wine. Poetry you've written. Or a chick flick. These are the way to a woman's heart." She patted his arm and tottered down the walk. Her cane waved over her white head. "If you need more love advice, you know where I live."

Freakin' hell. Now I've got an octogenarian giving me romance tips.

He returned to the shrubbery in front of his townhouse to untangle the Christmas lights from his ladder. Something purple caught his eye and he remembered Einstein dropping an object. He scooped it from the grass. A purple lace thong. A vision of Becca wearing it with her long legs wrapped around his waist dashed from his mind to his cock. *And I've got a damned dog luring me into his mistress' panties.*

****

Michael Bublé crooned Christmas music from the stereo while Becca sat at her desk. The empty blog template on her computer screen begged for words. She glanced at the clock and moaned. She'd been sitting there for twenty minutes, staring at her monitor, while her mind replayed every second of her interaction with Wolf in his front yard earlier. What was it about him? The way he looked? Which was damn sexy. The way he talked to her? Which alternated between annoying and—she sighed—damn sexy. She didn't want to think about the way he kissed or the magical things his tongue did to her mouth—even though she could barely think of anything else. *Girl, you need to get a grip.*

Enough day-dreaming and mooning over a man. Hadn't they all brought pain to her life in one form or another? First her dad walked out on her and her mom when things got bad, then Tommy Ray. Things hadn't been always bad between them, though. Not like it had been for her parents. Both of them had good jobs and were healthy and active. But Tommy Ray had gone searching online. For what, she wasn't sure. Neither was he, or so he claimed. "It just happened," he'd stated over and over—and with no remorse whatsoever.

"Men," she growled.

Einstein opened his eyes, yawned and licked his balls.

"Lucky you. You get to do what every man wishes he could." She sipped her lukewarm hot chocolate and winced. "By the way, mutt-meister, you better leave my thongs alone." Einstein stopped licking and raised his head. "I mean it. Stay out of my underwear drawer. Just my luck that I get a dog who teaches himself to open drawers. There are teeth marks around my dresser handles." The dog whined and went back to loving his testicles.

She returned her attention to her blog. What could she title her post to snag her audience's attention? Her fingers commenced typing: *Man-whore Has A Name.*

Okay, now what should his moniker be? She didn't want to use his real name. For all his rude and pawing nature, she'd never disclose Wolf's true identity. She opened her post with a paragraph telling how her dog had broken loose from her grasp to introduce himself to her new neighbor. A slow smile spread and she chuckled. She knew just the name.

Man-whore extended his hand, his gaze roaming my tight, sweaty running clothes. "Hello, my name is Dan Bullass. Folks just call me Bull." He favored me with his smarmy smile. Personally, I assumed most people would have gone with the last part of his name but, hey, that's just me.

Bull pushed up the sleeve of his yellow T-shirt—the front emblazoned with "I'm too sexy for this shirt"—to show me his tattoo. I'm telling you, ladies, you'd have rolled your eyes. A charging bull with red smoke coming from its nostrils, and every time man-whore flexed his impressive bicep, the bull's hind legs kicked out. It was a sight to behold, believe me.

Becca covered her mouth with her hands and chuckled at her work of fiction. She'd never done this before. Her blogs were usually a factual slice of her life. Never made up or a blatant exaggeration. She read over it again and nodded. Now what?

Bull walked Einstein and me to our door. "I'm having a party tonight. I'm celebrating the best day in the history of womankind." He leaned in and lowered his voice in a practiced sensual manner. "My birthday."

Then he had the audacity to wink at me. Did I go to his party? Yes, I did. And I'll be blogging about that tomorrow.

Great ending hook, Becca old girl. She added clip art of a bull pawing the earth and pressed the Publish button. She stood, stretched and glanced out of her window. Wolf had an air compressor running, inflating three large angels in his front yard. Evidently he wanted to decorate outside before his family came over for hot chocolate and cookies prior to their singing carols tonight.

Why angels? She scoffed. The man might be a lot of things, but prone to angelic behavior he wasn't.

She headed for the kitchen. Maybe she'd make a taco salad for dinner and eat it out on her back patio. Or she could see if his invitation to join his family tonight still stood. No, that would be a bad idea. Hadn't she just told him to leave her alone? Einstein started barking and scrambled for the front door as the bell rang. She pivoted, hurrying through the hallway to see who was there. A young man stood on her porch holding a floral arrangement of red and white carnations accented with sprigs of pine. Three plastic angels on sticks were positioned throughout the flowers.

"Ms. Sinclair?"

"Yes."

He extended the arrangement to her. "Happy Holidays." When he stepped off her porch and headed back to the blue delivery van, he saluted Wolf. And darn if her neighbor didn't salute him in return. What was that about?

She closed the door, set the flowers on her desk and removed the little card from the envelope. "'For the prettiest woman on Seashell Lane. W.' Who the heck is 'W'?" She glanced out of her bay window to Wolf's front yard and the three angels decorating it. "Oh, *surely* not."

Her fingertips trailed over the spicy, fragrant blooms as she struggled to accept the implications of Wolf's message on the card. Was this an attempt at flirting? She wasn't ready for another man in her life, no matter how he made her insides tremble with a look or a smile or a kiss. This past year had been twelve painful months of gaining her bearings. No, she still had some healing to do before she opened her heart to a man. Plus, she had to get through the holidays without dwelling on how horrendous they were last year.

Twenty-thirteen had nearly destroyed her.

Perhaps it had.

The giggling Becca her friends all loved had been replaced by a crabby, cynical, complaining woman. At the top of her New Year's resolution list was "find giggling Becca."

Maybe by next October she would.

Chapter 6

Becca had been in an aggravated mood all day, her mood darkening by the minute, like an impending hurricane blowing in from the Gulf. Wolf had her emotions on a continual swirl as he slowly drove her to madness. Every time she turned around, he was leaving her presents—and she didn't like it. How could she keep the perpetual scowl on her face if he kept charming her?

The day after she received the flowers, he'd pinned a Christmas stocking on the pine wreath hanging on her front door. Tucked inside the stocking were four pairs of red and green holiday-themed thongs and Godiva chocolates. *The dickwad.*

The next morning a box of cream-filled donuts sat at the top of her porch steps, waiting for her sweet tooth—and just *how* did he know they were her favorite? He'd scrawled across the top of the container "These aren't nearly as sweet as your kisses." The man must have thought her a sentimental fool if he expected her to fall for that sad line. She'd have kicked them to the curb if they hadn't been from her favorite bakery.

A bag of doggie treats and a toy for Einstein hung on her doorknob the next day—a dirty trick if you asked her, using her dog to get in her good graces.

This morning, a goofy card was taped to her front door asking her to dinner and a movie tonight. Wolf seemed determined to win her approval, but why, when he'd made no secret of his dislike of reporters?

In contrast, she shouldered a strong case of blame for mislabeling him as a man-whore on her blog. She grimaced. How was she to know all the women going in and out of his house were his sisters and sister-in-law? No doubt she should have clarified things in a post, but with her readership growing because of her popular rants about him, she continued the pretense. Her culpability was somewhat assuaged by calling him Bull instead of Wolf, thereby keeping his true identity a secret. As a writer, she could create humorous, snarky fantasy out of almost every movement Wolf made—and didn't women like fantasy?

She snatched several bags of toys off the passenger seat of her car, turned toward the sidewalks leading to the townhouses and groaned.

Evidently Wolf hadn't worked today for he'd added another blown-up decoration to his ever-growing menagerie of inflatable lawn ornaments. His front yard was a mishmash of cheap holiday embellishments. Where had this nutso found the room? She eyed his newest addition and gritted her teeth so hard her jaw ached.

Someone please tell me what an air-filled heart held by a bear has to do with Christmas?

Weren't the three angels singing the same chorus over and over sufficient for yard decorations? Or the two deer with their heads bobbing out of beat with said angel music? Or the eight-foot-tall snowman waving next to the six-foot Santa. Wasn't that enough?

Her gaze slid to the green, blow-up, evil-looking Grinch with eyes that glowed yellow in the night. Jammed beside it, Santa wore shades and rode a motorcycle. She sneered. A Harley, no less. Animated elves worked at a toy bench and a pack of blown-up wolves ran between his and her sidewalks. Inflatable candy canes and round ornaments the size of basketballs hung from his porch roof. Dozens of strands of lights were strung around every porch pillar and window and across his part of the roof to highlight

Santa in his sleigh pulled by eight reindeer.

What a hideous mayhem of decorations.

Thank goodness only eighteen days remained in December.

She carried the presents she'd bought for the Fireman's Toy Ride inside and removed them from the bags. On her dining-room table she placed an assortment of newborn and Barbie dolls, several jewelry-making kits, action figures, books, art sets and heaps of little cars and trucks. She'd wrap them this evening while she made cookies—and live off soup and tinned tuna for the next month or so to pay for the gifts.

After taking Einstein for a quick walk in the backyard, Becca hurried outside to tackle the large box in her trunk. The salesman at the hardware store had groaned and grunted when he'd loaded the carton containing the six-foot-high wooden bookshelves into her car. Seeing him struggle with it worried her. Frankly, she hadn't given any thought to how heavy the box would be for her to drag it inside.

She untied the rope securing her trunk lid over the long box and contemplated the best way to remove the carton and get it inside to her living room. How difficult could it be? She wrapped an arm around the box and pulled, hoping to hug it to her side.

It barely budged. *Crap!*

Shoving the sleeves of her sweatshirt to her elbows, she put every ounce of strength into the job. She tugged and pulled enough of the carton out of the trunk to allow gravity to upend it onto the street. Then she straightened, shifted her shoulders and used her sleeve to swipe the perspiration from her forehead.

She bent at the knees, put her shoulder to it and lifted the heavy item on an exhale and a loud grunt. Becca staggered under the weight across her shoulder. Maybe this wasn't such a good idea. The unmanageable carton wove her back and forth. For a few seconds, all she could do was stagger.

She made it up the step of the curb to the sidewalk, nearly dropping to her knees with the effort. Thigh muscles quivering with the strain of the weight, she gritted her teeth. "Come on, Becca, you can do this."

Thank goodness the walkway was only twelve feet long. She tried not to think of the three steps to her porch. Maybe she could drag or push the box up the steps—if she reached them under all this weight.

A loud rumble roared down the street and her stomach clenched at the familiar sound. Wolf's Harley eased to the curb.

"Becca! Don't. I'll carry that in for you."

She pivoted to tell him she didn't need or want his help. The sudden movement threw her load off balance. Arms clasped around the box, she fell backwards and her spine slammed on the hard ground. Air whooshed from her lungs on impact. A loud pop sounded as the box thudded across her face. Pain exploded in her nose and head.

"Becca! My God." A set of thick knees pushed into her side. "Here, let me get this off you." Wolf shoved the box away as if it were no heavier than a bag of tinsel. "Give me a chance to get this helmet off." Leather rustled and squeaked.

Wet warmth flowed over her lips.

"Oh, sweetheart, it looks like your nose is broken." Strong fingers moved from the bridge of her nose to its tip. The pain made her eyes cross. "Hold on. Let me get my first-aid kit."

His heat disappeared and running footfalls sounded on his porch. Slowly the spinning stopped, and she blinked to bring the world back into focus. Was her face smashed? She gingerly fingered her forehead, nose and cheeks and grimaced when she pulled back a blood-covered hand.

Einstein was barking like crazy from inside her townhouse. Bless his canine heart; he knew she needed him.

Wolf settled on his knees beside her again. "Some people bleed more than others when their noses break. Don't be alarmed." His voice was calm and authoritative as he snapped on latex gloves. Cool alcohol wipes were gently pressed across her face.

"Ith my noth broken?" My God, was that *her* voice? Why was she speaking with a lisp?

He shined a light in her eyes. "Good retina response." Chocolate eyes lowered to within inches of hers, minty breath swept across her face and a lock of dark hair fell across his forehead. The corners of his mouth twitched as if he were trying not to smile. "And, yes, sweetheart, your *noth* is broken. I'll do my best to set it so it's still pretty and straight."

"Thet it? No!"

Einstein's barking and whining increased. No doubt he sensed her anxiety.

Wolf gave a nonchalant shrug. "Set might be an extreme word. I'm just going to make sure it's straight."

"Are you two at it again?" Mrs. Minelli's orthopedic shoes came into view. "Oh no! She's bleeding! Shall I call an ambulance? I can press the button on my senior alert necklace." She held out a medical medallion strung on a silver chain around her neck. Today, her sweatshirt bore a Christmas-tree design with lights that somehow twinkled on and off.

"Thanks, Mrs. Minelli, but I've got it covered. I'll stop the bleeding and carry her inside."

"What happened?" The elderly woman tapped his side with her cane. "Did you belt her because she wouldn't get frisky with you?"

Wolf's hands stilled and he exhaled an audible sigh-fluttering the hair at Becca's temple. His tension was palpable. Under his breath, he muttered, "God, just give me some frickin' patience here." Then he aimed his thousand-watt smile at the older lady and told her what had happened.

"Well, okay then. I was just going to hitch a ride with Mrs. Bernstein to water aerobics. We broads need to keep our girlish figures. Becca, darlin', I'll check in on you tomorrow."

"Thank you." Her words trailed after the tottering old woman, her cane tapping as she meandered down the sidewalk.

Wolf's fingertips firmly pressed into her nose and more stars

43

exploded behind her eyes.

"Don't touch my noth!" She batted away his hands.

"Do you want to be called 'witch's beak' for the rest of your life?"

"Witheth beak? Ith it that bad?" What would her coworkers at the paper think? Still, did this yay-hoo know what he was doing? "If my noth needth to be thet, I want a profethenal to thet it."

He tore open a paper packet and removed two gauze cylinders. "I had advanced corpsman training in the Navy before I was recommended for the SEALs. Believe me, I've handled worse than a broken nose."

Wolf shoved the gauze up her nostrils.

More fireworks exploded in her head.

"Ow! You big thithead. You hurt me on purpoth." Her one hand tightened in a fist. If he hurt her again, she was going to belt him.

Those brown eyes of his shone with humor. "Thithead? We hardly know each other well enough for such intimacies." He smiled and tilted his head. "Although, I am getting pretty familiar with your taste in underwear. Einstein left a purple thong beside my ladder the day I fell off and another leopard-print set at my back door yesterday."

"Oh, no," she groaned. She'd never had trouble with her dog running off until this man moved in next door. She could see why a woman might chase after Wolf—an enticing blend of machismo, good looks and an unexpected measure of gentleness—but why was her dog so damned attracted to him? And just *why* was her dog so suddenly set on stealing her underwear?

"What did you do with my thongth? You never brought them back."

"Tied them to the handle grips of my Harley." He jerked his thumb over his shoulder.

"You *what!*" She would kill him.

His head leaned back as deep laughter erupted. "Don't get riled, sweetheart." His eyes bore humor and something akin to affection.

That damned box must have broken my mind.

44

"Thop calling me 'thweatheart.'"

"Can't." His fingers were more gentle on her face now. "It's part of my plan. Maybe if I keep calling you sweetheart, you'll start getting sweet on me."

"Cold day in hell, buthter."

"Do you have pain anywhere?"

"I think my back might be broken. I heard thomething pop when I fell."

Wolf's hands stilled. "Are you in pain, baby?" His dark eyebrows furrowed. "Move your fingers for me. Good. That's good." He shifted to her feet and wrapped his hands around her sneakers. "Push your toes into my hands. Excellent. Now your heels. Good. Good." His fingers slowly worked their way up her legs, probing, exploring.

"Thop feeling my legth."

"I'm checking for broken bones."

His hands squeezed her thighs, and she shot him a dirty look. "You're copping a feel, you thexth fiend."

His arrogant gaze swept to hers, warming her from the inside out. "Are you enjoying my touching you?"

"Thertainly not." *Well, maybe just a teeny-tiny bit.*

"Then I'm not copping a feel. When I do, you'll enjoy it. Believe me." His hands swept over her ribs in an expert manner.

"You pompouth jerk. You are tho full of yourthelf."

"And you're so cute when you're miffed about something. Which I've gotta admit is most of the time." Evidently satisfied she had no broken bones, he rolled her slightly and peered under her back. "I found the source of the popping."

"Oh?"

He heaved a sigh. "Yeah, you killed one of my wolves."

To Becca's surprise, Wolf scooped her into his arms and carried her up the steps to her door, as if she weighed no more than a hummingbird. "I'll get you inside and put some ice on your face. You know you're going to have two big shiners from the box's

45

impact."

"Thiners? You mean black eyeth?" *No, please, no!* She had two interviews for the newspaper tomorrow.

He stopped at her door and peered down at her. Those brown eyes of his danced with humor. "Yes, *black eyeth*." He shifted, raising his knee to help balance her as he reached to open her door. Einstein danced and whined and sniffed her to make sure she was okay.

Her pride stung from his remark. "I don't enjoy being made fun of."

His boots clomped on the wooden floor of her hallway. "I'm not making fun, sweetheart. What I'm trying to do is lighten your mood a little. You always take everything so seriously. Just for once, I'd like to see you smile."

He settled her on the sofa, tugged her grandma's afghan off the back of the sofa and covered her. Even on a mild day like today, the soft apricot-and-yellow knitted "comfort blankie," as grandma called it, brought its own consolation.

"Be right back. I'm going for ice packs, aspirin and my toolbox. You're not up to putting the bookshelves together this afternoon."

"You're right. I'm not. Thankth for your help." She sighed, thinking of how she'd never have gotten out from under that heavy box. "And for taking care of me too."

He turned and crouched next to the sofa. His warm hand covered one of hers. Einstein licked them both, and Wolf laughed deeply, the husky rumble touching the loneliness inside her. "Sweetheart, I don't mind taking care of you and my thong buddy here. I do think our movie date for tonight will have to be postponed. Bright theater lights wouldn't be good for your headache. We'll do it another time, okay?"

"Okay. Today ithn't turning out like I planned. I wath going to make Chrithmath cookieth later for the neighborth."

He trailed a fingertip down her cheek. "Were you going to make some for me too?" Oh, those brown eyes of his and the lone dimple that winked when he smiled. She nodded, and the movement of her head made her stomach lurch. "I thuppothe a cookie or two." This attraction was so not good. Hadn't she learned any lessons from her marriage? Men equaled pain.

He leaned over her and feathered his warm lips across her forehead. "Oh, sweetheart, my appetites go way beyond a couple cookies."

Her insides did a feminine freefall. *I just bet they do.*

"Stay here." He stood. "I'll get you those aspirins and something frozen for your face." Einstein followed Wolf out of the room.

"Wolf?"

His dark head peeked around the arched doorway. "Yeah?"

"I want my thongth back. No woman wanth her underwear turned into a bikerth trophy, ethpethally a Harley rider."

Wolf stared at her for a beat, and his eyes narrowed. "Bite me." He stalked out, slamming the door behind him.

God he was cute when she pushed his buttons. For the first time since Tommy Ray walked out on her, she laughed until her sides hurt.

Chapter 7

Ten minutes later, Becca lay with a sack of frozen peas over her face, peeking out from under the Green Giant on the bag to watch the muscular giant on her living room floor, methodically positioning every board and hardware item across the carpet.

Einstein alternately pranced from her to Wolf, spending more time wagging at their guest than snuggling with her.

Becca could appreciate the dog's interest. She had a fair share of it herself... like the way Wolf's jeans, buttery soft with age, hugged his thighs and butt. In fact, her hands itched to cup his mighty fine behind. She pinched her eyes shut and then winced. *Oh, girl, don't even go there.*

Wolf's head rose as if he'd noticed her facial movement beneath the bag of peas. "Those Tylenol taking care of the pain?"

"Uh-huh." They weren't taking care of the desire, though. She hadn't wanted a man this much in well over a year. Why now? Why him, of all people?

"What do you like on your pizza?"

"What?" She lifted the bag of peas. He held his cell in one large hand, his gaze focused on her. Was he inviting himself for dinner? The man was putting together her shelves. The least she could do was feed him. "I could cook."

"After what just happened to you out there? Nonsense. You

need to rest." One dark eyebrow rose. "Toppings?"

A shudder of awareness sashayed through her system when her eyes met his. Oh my, those piercing eyes of his and the way they studied her. It was almost as if he could see right into her soul.

"Ah…muthroom and ethtra cheeth."

Wolf dialed and joked with the person on the other end of the line. "You want my order or not, you degenerate slime ball?" His laughter, loud and booming, just like him, ricocheted off the walls. "Give me an extra-large pizza. Heap everything on one half and mushrooms and extra cheese on the other." He forked the fingers of one hand through his shoulder-length hair. "Yeah, I'm sharing it." His gaze swept to hers and a slow, badass smile made her insides flutter. "That's for me to know, buddy. It's someone I've been trying to charm for a few days."

She jerked the bag of peas off her face, her eyes narrowed at his implication.

He winced as he studied her expression. "How's it goin' with her? Ah…not so good." He picked lint off his black Harley T-shirt in a self-conscious gesture. After he gave the person on the other end her address, he slipped his cell into his pocket.

She rose on her elbows, her head pounding with the effort. "Who…who were you juth talking to?"

Suddenly he was very busy. A broad shoulder lifted. "Ah, my cousin, Vinny."

"Great, my life ith juth like a bad movie."

"Hey, that was a great flick. Ever see it? My sisters loved it."

She pressed the peas back over her face and reclined against the pillows. "No."

"I'll bring it over some night, and we can watch it together."

"No." She was not letting this man into her life any more than she had already.

Evidently he chose to ignore her reply. "I see you haven't decorated for Christmas yet."

"I have too. Thee my pointhetta on the coffee table?" She pointed to the angels and carnations on her desk. "Thank you for thoth. You thurprithed me."

He gave her a slow, sexy-as-hell smile and then winked. Damn, if all her female parts didn't wink right back.

What *was* she talking about? Oh yeah, decorations. "Thee my tree in the corner?"

He snorted. "That's not a tree. It's a plastic branch with tiny look-a-like ornaments clinging to it for dear life."

"Ith a tree. I thuppoth you've got a giant one in your houth, juth dripping with ornamenth."

"Damn straight."

"I hate arrogant men."

"So I've noticed." He started assembling the shelves. "How long have you been divorced?"

"A while. Tommy Ray moved out Chrithmath Eve."

"Christmas Eve?" Muscles rippled over Wolf's back as he screwed some pieces together. "What an asshole, ruining your holiday like that."

An old pain paid her heart a visit. This time, like a weakened tropical storm, it barely touched down. A slow smile spread. Was she finally getting over her divorce? Maybe Christmas wouldn't be so bad after all.

"How about you? Any etheth?"

He glanced over his shoulder, his forehead furrowed. "Etheth? Oh, exes." He smiled and nodded. "No. I was engaged while I was in the SEALs. It was too hard on her, never knowing where I was or what I was doing. At the drop of a hat or the chime of a text, I'd be gone and out of touch for months." He shrugged and turned back to the partially assembled shelves. "She married an accountant and has two rugrats now."

Had his fiancée hurt him the way Tommy Ray had her? Did he grieve her loss the way she did the man she'd once pledged herself to, supposedly 'til death do them part?

"I'm guessing you haven't dated since he left." His stayed hand

50

poised over the little piles of hardware until he evidently located what he needed and scooped it into his palm.

Talking to his back seemed easier than staring into his handsome face. "No. I've been too afraid. Being rejected or left behind hurth too much. Bethideth, men have thuth violent reactionth to thingth." Now why had she divulged anything so personal? Yet, sharing with him while he worked was comfortable, as if they'd done it a thousand times before. What was up with that?

His head whipped around and his dark eyes narrowed. "Did he hit you?"

How could she confess the shame of it? Although it had only happened twice, the abuse was very real. She shook her head and lied. "No, of courthe not."

"I've noticed the panicked look in your eyes whenever I get close." He tapped a screw with a hammer to get it started in a hole. "I wouldn't hurt you. That's not my style, especially after taking care of my sisters."

Now would be a good time to ask the questions that bothered her. "Why all the pretend? Why the change in attitude toward me?"

"Gotta admit the change didn't come easy. You've caused a lot of sleepless nights. On the bad side, thinking of you has put me in a pissy mood, or so Jace tells me." He shrugged, his back still facing her as he worked. "On the good side, my equipment at the station outshines everyone else's. Having inanimate objects to take my frustrations out on gave me time to think."

"About...?"

"About which was more important. Your feminine pull on me or my feelings toward reporters."

She worried her lower lip. "Wolf, I'm not thure I'm ready for anything. Ethpethally right before the holidayth." She wasn't looking forward to them after all the pain of last year's solitary existence.

He pivoted on the ball of his foot and slung one forearm over a muscular thigh. "You're dreading them, aren't you? You're welcome to join in on all the celebrations with me and my family. You'll have a good time. I promise."

"I already mithed your caroling night. How did it go?" She had stood at her window watching them all pile into their vehicles, laughing and teasing each other and, once more, felt on the perimeter of happiness.

A wide smile spread. "Went great. Two old geezers fell in love with Megan and tried to hit on her." He laughed. "The look on her face." He shook his head. "I wish you'd come along and join us for the rest of our celebrations."

The doorbell rang and Einstein raced to it, barking.

Wolf stood and looked at her. "No pressure. No obligation. I just hate the thought of you being alone during Christmas and New Year's."

On Wolf's command, Einstein returned to her side. After settling up with the delivery person, he carried in a large pizza box and a six-pack of beer, setting them on the coffee table. "My lady, dinner is served." He flipped back the lid and the aromas of onions, green peppers, sausage and pepperoni filled her living room.

"Lookth great." Her stomach growled. "I'll get plateth and napkinth." She stood and Wolf's hands settled at her waist. Her insides did a twitchy thing at his touch.

He tilted his head. "You're not dizzy, are you? I'm still concerned you might have a slight concussion."

"No. I'm fine." She shook her head twice and the room spun slightly. Waiting for her world to stop twirling, she focused on the dimple that blinked with his smile. What would it feel like to dip the tip of her tongue into the delicious little crevice? *Girl, don't even go there.*

Once she returned with their utensils, she sat and shoved pillows behind her back.

Wolf settled on the floor across from her. "I'm starved. This has to serve as late lunch and dinner. I helped Cassie decorate her beauty shop after I put up my latest addition out in the yard. Did you see the bear? Wendy Anne found him in a Goodwill store."

Yes, and she should have left it there. "Why tho many decorationth?"

He snapped off a top on one of the beers and handed it to her. "Mom was always crazy about Christmas. Guess I got it from her. Plus, after I left the SEALs to make a home for my sisters, things like decorating for the holidays became a fun thing for us. We'd go overboard, each of us trying to outdo the other." He opened his beer and took a long drag, his Adam's apple bobbing.

Becca sipped, pretending not to gawk. What was wrong with her? Since when did a man swallowing beer turn into such a sensual sight? She had the strangest urge to open her mouth over his windpipe, just to explore every nuance of movement with her tongue. *My God, I must have a concussion. I've gone insane.*

"Easy on the beer. We don't know if your stomach can handle a lot of liquid and food just yet."

"You juth want the whole pitha for yourthelf." She feigned annoyance as she placed a slice on her plate. There was too much attraction ricocheting through her system for this man, and to her shock it was growing at breathtaking speed. She was ensnared in a vortex of feelings, swirling and pulling her down for the count.

She didn't want to be attracted. She feared it. Yet, part of her was drawn to him. Perhaps it was his devotion to family and how he took his obligations to them so seriously. If only her dad and Tommy Ray had been half the men Wolf was in that regard. The man sitting across from her could be funny and caring, yet damned annoying. She'd do better to focus on the latter.

"The family is doing Christmas at my place this year. Usually Jace and Wendy Anne have it at their house, but I'm afraid of overtaxing the little momma."

"You're very protective." She bit into her pizza slice, enjoying the pull of cheese and slurping it in with her tongue.

Wolf stared at her for a beat or two, his brown eyes darkening. "God, you can even make eating pizza sexy."

53

She laughed. "What? What did I do?" The heat of a blush warmed her cheeks.

He shook his head and brought his second slice of pizza to his mouth, devouring half of it in one bite. Einstein laid his muzzle on Wolf's thigh and whined.

Hell, I'd whine, too, if I was lying across his massive thigh.

The object of her lust tugged a piece of pepperoni off the remaining portion of his slice and fed it to Einstein.

"Are you thtill playing Thanta thith weekend?" The thought of him dressed in a padded suit pulled at the corners of her mouth. How kissable would he be in a white beard and mustache?

His head bobbed. "Ready as I'll ever be. The ride is always fun. Getting people to donate toys for needy kids is a damn fine cause. No kid should do without, especially at Christmas."

"I know. You thould thee the toyth on my dining-room table. I can't wait for the ride. My Ninja wath in the garage getting a new tranthmiththon. I wath afraid it wouldn't be done in time."

He speared her with a glare, his beer bottle stopped halfway to his mouth. "You're not driving. If you insist on going, you can ride with me. But you're not getting on that crotch rocket so soon after hitting your head."

She slapped her pizza crust into the box. "Ith your hearing bad? 'Cauth if you thought I athked for your permithion, you damn well need it thecked."

His jaw clenched and his eyes narrowed. "No, I don't need my hearing thecked. But you'll need that fine ass of yours smacked if you try riding your bike in the next few days. For all we know, you might have a slight concussion."

"You keep thaying that. I'm fine." Who the hell did he think he was? Her keeper? Her master? Her…her…"I do not have a concuthon." Well, she did have that urge a few moments ago to taste his Adam's apple, but that wasn't so gawd-awful weird, was it?

Sensing her displeasure, Einstein jumped on the sofa beside her and she petted him.

"Don't fight me on this, sweetheart. Would riding on the back of my Harley be such a hardship?"

"I won't be bothed around. I'm my own woman. No man tellth me what to do."

He upended his beer and drained it. "God, I thought once I got the girls raised, I wouldn't have to hear this damn song and dance again. I'm only trying to look out for your welfare." With his dark gaze focused on her, he slid another slice of pizza on his plate. "Is it so horrible I don't want anything bad to happen to you?"

Well, when he put it that way…Riding with her arms wrapped around his waist wouldn't be such a hardship. It would serve him right if she dressed up as one of Santa's elves. *Now, there's a thought.* "Okay."

His sexy-as-hell smile creased his face. "You'll ride me?" He blinked and blushed. "I meant you'll ride with me?"

She grabbed another slice of pizza and ate. Best to just let all that riding business alone.

Once they were through eating, Wolf gathered the empty box, bottles and dishes and carried them to her kitchen. When he returned, he settled on the sofa next to her and put his arm around her shoulders. "I thought I'd get a little dessert before I finish those shelves."

Her mind flew over her inventory in the kitchen. "I've got ith cream."

His fingers trailed up her neck, and all her female parts took notice, just like they did every time he touched her. "Ice cream has its appeal, but it doesn't measure up to your soft skin." He tilted his head and pressed his lips to her neck, working his way up to the sweet spot behind her ear. She angled her head so he could reach it better.

"I'm glad we got that dating thing settled." He bit her ear and her breathing hitched.

"What…" she swallowed. "What dating thing?"

His teeth grazed her jawline and she wanted to whimper. Chills tap-danced across her skin and her nipples all but pirouetted.

"You and me." He breathed more warm kisses across her neck, and strong arms banded around her as he enveloped her in his potency.

"I...I didn't know we were dating."

He bit gently on her earlobe and then soothed it with his tongue. "Really?" He splayed his large hand between her breasts. "Didn't your heart tell you?"

Honest to Pete, the man had more moves and lines than the Miami Dolphins. She wouldn't be so easily swayed, no matter how he affected her—and he *did* affect her. "You've done a one eighty thinth your birthday party."

"That I have. I think you charmed me with all your scowls and attitude." He pressed his face to her neck, and his shoulders shook with laughter.

She punched his bicep. "You fool."

"That's what scares me. I could be a fool for you so easily." He stood and went back to assembling the shelves.

While he worked, they chatted about her going to college and his going into the Navy. He shared bits and pieces about his SEAL training. Before long, the shelves were completed. "Where do you want them?"

"Againth that thmall wall to the right of the dethk."

"You got it."

The muscles bunched across his back as he lifted the unit and positioned it in the center, just like she wanted. "Perfect."

"Will you fill this big thing with books or family pictures?"

"Bookth and my collection of butterflieth."

"You like butterflies, huh? Cassie collects angels. Jenna's really into sewing, so she collects antique thimbles. April likes cat figurines."

"What do you collect?"

A slow badass smile spread. "Harleys...and grumpy women."

Chapter 8

Wolf gathered the box and shipping materials from the shelves and carried them outside to the dumpster at the corner of their street. He took Einstein along for his walk. When he got back, Becca was upstairs and the shower was running.

If he knew her better, he'd join her. His gaze swept up the steps. She'd never forgive him if he pushed things between them. Better to keep to their original plan. He'd pick out a DVD while she got out of her blood-splattered sweatshirt and showered.

"Come on, Einstein. Help me pick out a good movie." He crouched in front of her entertainment unit and perused her DVD titles. "Bet all she's got are chick flicks. Hello…" He pulled a collection from the bottom shelf. "She's got the Bourne series. It's been a while since I've watched them."

He had *The Bourne Identity* queued up when Becca came down the steps. She wore yellow sleep shorts with blue frogs and a matching blue tank top. Her eyes were starting to color with bruising. "How's your head?" He glanced at his watch. "You could probably take a couple more Tylenol."

"I took thom already." She pressed fingertips to her forehead. "Hurth."

He placed his hands on her shoulders and slid them up and down her bare arms. God, she had soft skin. "You want me to go home so you can call it an early night?" If she sent him home, he'd only worry about her. She seemed a little unsteady on her feet. "How about if we snuggle on the sofa? I'll rub your back to help you relax."

She looked at him as if he'd suggested the impossible. "You'd do that?"

"Sure." He sat and removed his boots before sprawling on the sofa, positioning pillows behind his head so he could watch the movie. "Come here. Lay on top of me."

"On top of you?" A blush kissed her cheeks and desire punched his gut. For all her grumpiness, she charmed him. Hell, she'd done more than that; she'd burrowed herself into his mind. He couldn't stop thinking about her. Somewhere along the way a fierce protectiveness had sprouted and grown.

She twisted the hem of her sleep shirt. "I might be too heavy."

"Nonsense." He patted his chest and waited. "I guarantee you'll feel better." *I'll hurt like hell with you so close and yet untouchable, but I have a need to take care of you. And I'm not even going to try to analyze that.*

She pressed her knee into the edge of the sofa and straddled him. He held his arms out and she snuggled against his chest. Once he'd enveloped her, he exhaled a long, shaky breath. While his intentions were honorable, his cock was a sneaky bastard. That appendage was getting ideas, getting ready to rear its ugly head. He chuckled at his own sick joke.

"What?" She leaned her forearms into his chest and stared at him. God he loved the expressiveness of her eyes. Like, right now, curiosity sparked in them.

He shook his head. "Sweetheart, you do not want to know." His cock, though, wanted to join in the fun and started to grow. "Ah...just ignore that." *Shit.*

"Oh." She wiggled against him and smiled.

He gritted his teeth. "Becca. Have a heart. I'm trying to be good here."

To his surprise, she giggled. What a delightful sound. When she rubbed against him again, he growled. She had him fully aroused now.

His hand slid down the curve of her back and cupped her ass, pulling her even closer to increase the painful friction, something that hurt so dammed much he welcomed it. His other hand slid into her damp hair and fisted. Her minty breath floated over his face and her eyes widened.

He issued his warning. "If you don't behave, you'll be going down the dark side, broken nose or not. Now lie still, dammit." Sweat beaded on his forehead. He wanted her so badly, even his molars ached.

She tilted her head. "Dark thide? Are you into kink, Dan Wolford?"

Why did he feel as if he were being interviewed? "What I'm into at this particular moment is some serious lust. Now behave."

Golden flecks glowed in her hazel eyes. She trailed a finger down his jaw and the side of his neck. "Awl, ith the big bad Wolf afraid of the little wounded theep?" She was clearly in teasing mode. And damn if her temporary lisp wasn't as appealing as hell.

He rolled, tucking her under him. "There's an old German saying: He who makes himself a sheep will be eaten by the wolves."

"Oh, and will you eat me?" A vibrant blush stained her cheeks as the full implication of her words sunk in. She pinched her eyes shut and winced.

Her embarrassment charmed him and the thought of tasting her hardened him even more, if that were possible. "That could be arranged, sweetheart, when your head isn't pounding." He bit her jaw and soothed it with his tongue. His fingers slipped under her sleep shirt and feathered a trail across her warm, satin skin. "I don't want you to be in any discomfort when I make love to you. I'll want you focused on me, not a damn headache."

She tugged on his T-shirt and slipped her small hand under it to rub against his side. "You think I'll allow you to make love to me?"

He kissed her lips in a tentative move, trying his best not to bump her nose. "A man lives to hope." He gave what he hoped was his most disarming smile.

"I don't know if I'm ready for you." Her fingers moved across his chest and found his nipple. She toyed with it and he nearly lost all rational thought.

"You're playing with me, right?"

A smile tugged at her lips. "On the other hand, maybe I'm jutht a wolf in theep'th clothing." She waggled her eyebrows and giggled.

Well, look at her; she's got a sense of humor. Why does she keep it hidden? He kissed her beneath her ear and enjoyed her intake of breath, her shiver of awareness. "I read somewhere that a wolf gives his opinion and rests on it. He renders service where there is no reward. He resides in solitude as if things don't affect him. Not because he has no feelings, but because he has too much."

"Do you feel too muth? What thingth or people do you feel too muth for?"

Her hazel eyes regarded him and her hand covered the bulge of his pecs. There was a familiarity to her contact. Odd, since she'd never touched him before. Yet, his soul recognized it, reveled in it and bathed in its sustenance. Fear did a freefall over his spirit. *Dear God, I'm falling in love with her.*

"All this talk must be getting to your headache." His arm banded around her, he shifted onto his back, taking her with him so she once more laid sprawled over him. Remote in hand, he turned the volume on low. "Is that too loud?"

"No." She snuggled closer, smelling of vanilla and lilacs.

He slowly stroked a hand up and down her back. God, she felt good against him. Her hand remained over his heart, almost as if she knew she owned it. He rubbed his cheek across her hair and sighed in contentment.

The next thing he knew, credits were rolling on the screen. Becca's long legs were draped over his hips. His hand curled around her thigh while the fingers of his other hand were woven into her long red hair. Her gentle breathing was muffled against his neck. Einstein was sprawled across his feet. Wolf was cocooned with flesh, both human and canine. It wasn't such a bad thing. In fact, it felt damn good. It felt like home.

****

Sunlight streaming through the bay window woke Becca. Why was she in her living room? Why was her sofa snoring? Who had a hand tucked under her sleep shorts, curled around her bare ass? Her mind jarred awake. *Crap! I'm lying on Wolf. Did we sleep here all night?*

Had she overslept? She glanced at the clock on her desk and exhaled in relief. Seven oh nine. The first of her two interviews wasn't scheduled until ten. What about the man lying beneath her? Did he have someplace he had to be? Einstein nudged her elbow and whined.

She moved slowly, hoping she wouldn't wake her surprise overnight guest. As soon as she had the sliding glass door in her dining room opened a foot, Einstein bolted outside, across her deck and into the yard. He ran for his favorite palm tree and bid it a wet good morning before racing around the yard twice, sniffing his domain for intruding monsters. Once he was sure his backyard was secure, her guard dog raced back inside.

"Want some kibble, baby?" She snapped her fingers and he followed her into the kitchen. After filling one bowl with food, she rinsed his water bowl, scooped out a handful of ice cubes from the ice maker and added fresh water.

She padded back into the living room and climbed onto her man again. Her man. Didn't she wish? Where did that thought come from? Wasn't it just yesterday she was afraid to get close to him or any guy? *Get a grip, girl.*

"Wolf. Wolf, wake up."

His long, dark lashes fluttered a couple times before they

61

opened. A slow, sexy smile spread and her world went from morning grey to rainbow bright.

What the heck is wrong with me? Where's my control?

"Morning, sweetheart." A lock of his dark hair hung over his forehead. She pushed it back, surprised at the silkiness. His large hand slipped under her shorts and cupped her bottom just as it had in his sleep.

"You've got your hand on my ass."

"Yeah." He stretched one muscled arm over his head and yawned, seemingly quite pleased with himself. "And a mighty fine ass it is." Just for good measure, he squeezed it.

He also had a massive morning hard-on, but she wasn't mentioning that. She'd slept all night in his arms. With Tommy Ray demanding his room to sprawl out on the bed, they'd never lain with their limbs entwined. This was a first. Yet, snuggled against this man, she'd slept better than she had in years.

"Your lisp is gone."

"So it is." She hadn't noticed until he mentioned it.

"How's your head this morning?" Wolf's forehead was wrinkled in concern and she was touched once again by his caring nature. *Well, why the hell not.*

She cupped her hands around his face, enjoying the whisker stubble against her palms. "I feel wonderful."

His eyes widened when she leaned in and claimed his lips. She moved her mouth over Wolf's soft lips, angling her head so her nose wouldn't touch his. The hand on her bare backside opened and closed twice, before a masculine groan rumbled from deep inside. She rocked a couple times against his erection. Both of his muscular arms banded around her waist as he pressed kisses down her neck. "You better stop this while I still have some control left."

There, he'd done it again. He put her welfare ahead of his needs. Evidently, this was part of his personality. Hadn't he left the SEALs to take care of his family after their parents died in a fire? Was that why he became a fireman? To save the parents of other children so they wouldn't know the pain he and his siblings had? What was it he'd said last night about wolves? Something about rendering service where there was no reward? This altruistic man stood head and shoulders taller than any she'd ever known.

She kissed his chin and then both his eyes. "Do you have a condom?"

The emotions that played out on his face fascinated her. He was more complex than she'd imagined. Could she reach the part of him he kept so tightly caged, the part that desired for himself? What were his secret yearnings? Did he ever reveal them to anyone? Well, he would to her. She'd find them; dig deep into him until he showed her the real Wolf.

She ran her tongue over his lips and a tremble jogged through him. "Condom?"

He raised his hips and reached into his back pocket, tugging out his wallet. Where most men had pictures in plastic sleeves, he had foil packets. She compressed the flame of jealousy that scorched through her veins to singe her heart. How many women was he seeing that he needed to carry them like this?

His wallet hit the coffee table after Wolf retrieved one. He held the packet between his fingers and she snatched it from him.

"Before I put this on you, Dan Wolford, I want to make one thing clear. In my ignorance, I shared my ex-husband with other women. I won't share you. If you and I only last a week, it'll be one week where you're only having sex with me." She waved the condom at him. "Are we clear?"

Dark eyelashes blinked and seriousness smoothed Wolf's facial features. "Crystal." He forked fingers through his hair. "Get up."

Her heart dropped along with the condom he'd handed her. Had she pushed him too far? Demanded too much? Then so be it. Better to know now before she allowed her feelings to color the picture. She'd not be hurt or used again. She stood and waited for him to leave. Einstein trotted over and shoved his muzzle against her hand. The dog was so good at reading her emotions.

63

Her not-so-willing sex partner reached for his wallet and condom, shoving both into his back pocket. Her wounded feminine pride limped back to its hiding place.

With a resigned sigh, she shifted to her desk and fiddled with the flowers Wolf had sent her. *Well, so much for that. Looks like once more I'm not going to be woman enough to keep a guy from leaving.*

His hand snaked out and wrapped around her waist, pulling her to him. "Don't go so far. This deal goes both ways. I won't share you with anyone either." Her dog growled and Wolf smiled. "Okay, I'll acquiesce to you for the moment, Einstein." His dark gaze flitted back to her. "Look, sweetheart, I've got no problem with being exclusive, but what's happening between us will damn well last more than a week." He scooped her into his arms and carried her up the stairs.

"What are you doing?" She laughed, surprised at how happy she was at this particular second. He wasn't leaving. He was staying and by the way desire darkened his eyes, he was planning on doing delightful things to her. *Yay for me!*

"Tell your dog to stay. I'm not making love to you with his beady eyes watching. Our first time is going to be in a bed—alone, naked, sweaty and so damn into each other a nuclear blast could melt the roof off this place and we'd never notice."

Well, this was different. A speedboat of desire raced through her system. "Really?"

"Bet on it."

"Einstein, get on your chair and stay."

Chapter 9

Before Wolf carried her into the bedroom, he stopped and kissed her lips. God, she had a sweet mouth. "Close your eyes." If she saw her reflection in the mirror as he carried her to the bed, she'd freak. Both eyes were black. Hell, nearly her whole face was bruised. Even her lips bore a strange bluish tint.

"Why?" She smiled, her white teeth gleaming in a face dappled with bruises. Even in this marked state, her beauty nearly brought him to his knees. Her arms were wrapped around his neck and he inclined his head to kiss her shoulder.

"God, you're so beautiful. Close your eyes."

"Close my eyes?"

"Let me teach you how the absence of sight will heighten your other senses." He winked.

"Ah…okay." Her eyes snapped shut. "You won't hurt me?"

"Never. I promise." Why would she even ask such a thing? He kissed her forehead and set her on her feet next to the purple-covered bed. His gaze swept the room, hunting for something to use as a blindfold. A white scarf was draped over the corner of her dresser mirror. "Keep your eyes closed. No peeking." He snatched the end of the scarf, snapped it out and tied it around her eyes. "That's not too tight, is it? I don't want you in pain."

"No, it's fine."

"Good." He pushed her long hair aside and kissed the back of her neck. So soft. Her skin was so freakin' soft. He could devour her. Her smell, her taste, her satiny essence beckoned to him like a siren.

Her bedroom was a study in femininity. There were various shades of lavenders and purples in this space, showcasing white furniture. On a large nightstand sat two stacks of romance novels, if the bare-chested men on the covers were any indication. A forties vintage white phone, flowered notepad and feathered pen sat on the other side of a white lamp with crystal beads dangling from the bottom of the lampshade.

"You enjoy being a woman, don't you?"

A nervous laugh escaped. "It's what I am." She tensed beneath his fingers. "Wait, you're not into some kind of weird role play, are you? I'm not pretending to be a man for anyone."

He laughed. "No, baby, I'm not into that. I'm just looking around your room. Everything is so feminine and sensual. Just like you." Answering his acute need to touch her, he trailed fingers down her arms. "It smells like you too. Of vanilla and lilacs."

She shrugged. "One's room should reflect its owner. How does yours look?"

He wrapped his arms around her waist and pulled her back against his chest. "You'll find out tonight." He nipped her shoulder and studied the large black-and-white framed pictures of a younger Becca in leotards, dancing and leaping through the air.

"You're a dancer?" He was spellbound. Whoever had taken the photos had captured her grace and beauty and strength. "Damn, Becca. Why are you hiding these pictures up here? You should have them downstairs where everyone can see them."

"They're private. Taken before my dad left us, when my life was happy and secure." Her voice wavered.

All his questions about her past would have to wait for another time. For now, he and his lady had needs. He placed his hands on her shoulders and turned her around. Taking her hands, he placed them at the bottom of his shirt. "Pull this off me, sweetheart."

"At last, I get to do something. You know, this isn't fair. You get to see me, but I can't see you." She leaned in and kissed his chest. He hardened more, if that were possible.

"You can touch me and taste me. Tonight I'll take the blindfold." He cupped her face and kissed her lips. "Tonight you can make me as vulnerable as you feel right now."

She lifted a shoulder. "Well…I suppose your idea has some merit."

Her beautiful, bruised face tugged at his heart. "Sweetheart, why don't you take off your shirt? I might knock your nose. Sometimes I can be what Mom used to refer to as a bull in a china shop."

She grimaced at his words. "Bull?"

He could have sworn her bruises paled before she blushed. Grasping the hem of her shirt, she slowly pulled it over her head, and Wolf's heart went on strike.

"My God, sweetheart. You're beautiful." Her full, round breasts were tipped with the purest pink he'd ever seen and he longed to touch and kiss and suck them. She cupped her breasts to hide them, a movement that aroused him even more, if possible. He'd made her uncomfortable and that disturbed him. Maybe if he was less vocal and concentrated more on giving her pleasure. He pulled a hand from a breast and pressed a kiss to her palm. "I have to be the luckiest man on this planet."

He released her hand and feathered fingertips up her arm. Her lips parted and the pulse at her slender throat increased. His fingertips continued their journey across her shoulder blades as he stepped behind her. "Skin like porcelain."

Sweeping her long auburn hair aside, he pressed three kisses to the back of her neck. There was a subtle intake of her breath. He rained more kisses across her shoulder. "You're like satin and silk. A man could die touching you…" he trailed the tip of his tongue down the graceful arch of her spine, "…tasting you. But believe me, the dying man would count his life as one well-lived."

He hoped to hell that he was that guy.

Slowly, he turned her around and tipped his forehead to touch hers, his hands at her waist. "There will never be another woman like you. Never." His lips covered hers and her mouth opened to him. His tongue delved in to lay claim and possess, for this woman would damn well be his. He'd never imagined himself to be the kind of man to fall so quickly, but fallen he had. Now the most important objective in his life was winning and keeping her love.

Wolf backed her to the bed, thrust one hand into her hair and fisted the silken strands. The other slid around her back and slipped under her shorts to clasp the perfect curve of her ass. Her arms wrapped around his waist and sharp nails scraped his back. Tremors of need surged through him. If he didn't step back and slow down, he'd be inside her before her back even hit the mattress. That wasn't what he wanted. Their first time had to be special. Memorable. Mutually satisfying.

"Lie down, baby." He used her movement to his advantage and slipped off her sleep shorts as she stretched out on her bed. "Give me a sec." He tugged his wallet from his jeans and laid it open on the nightstand, removing two foil packets before shedding his jeans and socks. Then he snagged a long string of pearls from her dresser. Belts hung from a lace-covered hanger on her closet door, and he removed two of them.

"What are you doing?" Becca shifted on the bed, obviously nervous and trying to listen to his movements.

"Setting the scene."

"Candles?"

"Belts."

"What?"

He hooked two leather belts together. "You need to learn to trust me. To trust I won't ever hurt you, and to do that I need to make you more vulnerable than you've ever been with anyone else. I'm going to tie your wrists over your head. If that thought freaks you out, tell me. I'll stop." The military operated on much the same principle. Tear personnel down to their lowest and then build them back up again. He had no intention of being quite so extreme, just taking away a measure of control so she would finally feel safe in his care. He sensed her shocked glare from beneath the blindfold. "Becca, I won't hurt you."

She licked her lips, her breathing more rapid. "You're going to tie my hands?"

"Unless you tell me otherwise." He waited. This had to be her decision or she'd never trust him.

Her swallow was audible within the silence of the room. "O... okay."

He straddled her hips, leaned down and gently kissed her lips. "Good choice. Now, clasp your hands and place them above your head on the pillows." Making a loop in the belts, he placed it over her wrists and tied a loose knot around one of the spindles on the headboard with the other end. "Comfy?"

"I get to do this to you tonight. Right?" She sounded a little pissed, as if she weren't overly thrilled with being blindfolded and tied up.

He reached for the strand of pearls. "Sweetheart, you can do anything you want to me. Anytime." He palmed the jewelry. "I want you to concentrate on your sense of touch. You won't be able to see what I'm doing to you, but your other senses will pick up the slack." He held the pearls near her ear and opened and closed his hand. "What do you hear?"

"A rattling. Wolf, what does any of this have to do with sex? All I was after was a morning quickie."

He leaned over and whispered next to one ear while softly moving the pearls next to her other, rubbing the beads together. "I want you to be aware of all your senses when I make love to you—whether it's slow, sweet love or fast, passionate, up-against-the-wall sex. From now on, you'll be aware of everything and take nothing for granted."

She turned her head toward him and he outlined her lips with his tongue. He trailed the necklace over the inside of her arm. She jerked.

"Pearls. Feel their warmth?"

She licked her lips. "Yes."

He skimmed the beads over her face, neck and breasts. "The skin of your throat and chest has a pearly white glow. These poor things don't stand a chance of measuring up to your beauty. I'm going to run my fingertips over one breast and your pearls over the other. Can you feel the difference?" Her skin quivered under his touch, sending a jolt of desire through him. He wanted to please her like no other man before him and, in that moment, he knew he wanted to be the last man to ever touch her in this way. He wanted her—and he wanted her to want him in equal measure.

"Which breast is being touched by my fingers?"

She arched and sighed. "Don't know. You better touch me some more." The corners of her delectable mouth quirked in a smile.

Oh, she was a delight, she was. "You wouldn't be teasing me, would you?"

"Aren't you teasing me, big guy?"

"I've only begun." He lay the pearls aside and reached for the feather pen. Turning it around, he flicked the feather beneath the curve of her breast and across her nipple. Her mouth opened slightly as her nipple peaked even more. "Every time you use your pen from now on, you'll think of the naughty ways I've used it." He moved to her side and trailed it down her stomach. "Naughty?" Her voice had a breathy quality which hardened him to the point of madness.

He flicked the feather across the tops of her thighs near their juncture and she arched again. "Oh, yeah, baby. Naughty." Tossing the feather aside because, really, why should it have all the fun, he scooted farther down the bed and began kissing her ankles. Slowly he worked his way up her toned legs, inhaling her scent and loving every inch of her satiny smooth skin with his hands and lips.

When he reached the apex of the most luscious pair of legs he'd

70

ever had the pleasure of tasting, her moans were a real turn-on, shooting a rush of hot blood to his groin. Still, it was nothing compared to her writhing and fisting of the comforter when he feasted on her. With the second stroke of his tongue, she climaxed. The shriek of his name tumbling from her lips was something he'd not soon forget. He stayed with her, giving her tender kisses and touches until the spasms receded.

Then he undid the belt and removed her blindfold. "I need your hands on me, baby. And I want to watch your eyes while I make slow love to you." He rubbed her wrists, kissing the tender skin at her pulse points. "Do you trust me now?" He cupped her beautiful face in his hands. Like topaz jewels, her eyes fixed upon his. "Have I convinced you I'd never do anything to hurt you? I could overpower you in a heartbeat. Yet, I never would. I care too much." He kissed her, pouring out all the novel, powerful emotions that had rocketed through him the moment he touched her the night of his birthday party. "I care." He kissed her again, long and languid. "I care."

Touching and tasting her had him more aroused than ever before. He reached for a packet on the nightstand, opened it and sheathed himself.

Becca stroked and rubbed as she took her turn exploring his body. Every touch of her hands shoved him closer to the edge of release. He wanted to plunge into her warmth, yet he willed himself to take things slow.

She bit his nipple before sucking it and his eyes crossed. "I can't believe you took all that time with me."

A freckle on her jaw drew his attention and he kissed it. "A man doesn't devour a gourmet meal; he savors it." He nipped the same place on her jawline. "He nibbles."

"Leave it to you to equate sex with eating."

He chuckled. "Well now, sweetheart, there is *that.*"

A slow smile spread and he was charmed. He leaned over her to whisper sensual thoughts in her ear while his hand took a long, slow journey of her body. He rained kisses over her neck and chest, kissing her breasts before drawing one pink nipple into his mouth. She moaned his name, weaving her fingers into his hair to hold him to her.

She shifted on the bed. "Wolf, I need you inside me."

He rose on his forearms over her and stared into her hazel eyes, more golden now than green. She reached between them and guided him inside her warmth, welcoming him home in the sweetest way possible. He took her hands, entwined their fingers and placed them over her head, and slowly began to make her his own.

Chapter 10

Becca was five minutes late for her interview with the owner of Wave of Sensuality. She'd been prepared to pull the old 'traffic was heavy' excuse, but the moment Ariel Martine, owner of the boutique, took one look at her bruised face, being late was forgotten.

The dark-haired woman placed a gentle hand to Becca's cheek. "My God, girl! Who did this to you?"

She laughed. "Not who. What. I was trying to carry a huge box of bookshelves into the house by myself. My hunky neighbor pulled up on his Harley and I lost my balance."

Ariel nodded with a knowing gleam in her eye. "Uh-huh. Just how hunky is this guy?"

Just as she'd sighed over and over on her way here, she exhaled another one for Ariel. "He carried me inside, took care of me and held me in his arms all night."

An arm slipped around Becca's waist and Channel #5 wafted over her. "You interview me first. Then I'm gonna interview you, and I'm betting I get the better story."

Oh, girlfriend, if you only knew.

Becca's gaze swept around the boutique. "Oh my, this looks like sin heaven."

"Come." Ariel made a beckoning motion. "Let me show you

around. I have so many last-minute items for men to buy their women. I'm doing something new this year." She handed Becca an iPad. "Enter your name into the gift registration form. It's a wish list like newlyweds use, only my female customers list items they'd like their significant other to purchase, complete with the correct sizes."

"What a neat idea. Men are so clueless about sizes."

Ariel laughed and pointed. "Go ahead, enter your name. With a man in your life, you might as well avail yourself of this service. I mean, you have that glow about you, as if you've been loved recently and well."

Indeed she had. Her body still hummed from Wolf's touch—inside and out. "What if a lady registers and no one shops here for her?"

"While that does happen, I find most men are eager for the help. Men love pleasing their women, do they not?" Her finely waxed eyebrow arched. "And, of course, there's no obligation."

Becca complied and entered her name and sizes. She also added a few sexy lingerie items, just in case. One barely-there item was a passionate purple and silver teddy, which had been designed to lift and emphasize the breasts. Its best feature, Ariel pointed out, was the lace-lined slit in the crotch if a man couldn't wait to get to the Promised Land.

When she left, she had the makings for a very nice newspaper article *and* two pair of crotchless panties and matching bras. She'd wear the emerald set tonight and save the black one for later.

Her second interview was across town with Slash Harper, the owner of Demons and Dolls Toy Store on Pinella. Slash was not as engaging as Ariel. In fact, something about him gave Becca the creeps. Was it the aura of his store? Or his eerie name.

He kept pointing out his large inventory of demon and military action figures and dolls of every type, offering curt answers to her questions whenever she questioned him about his holiday specials. Although he did nothing wrong, he set off alarm bells and whistles in her reporter's mind.

When she stepped out into the sunlight, a sign a few doors up on the strip mall caught her attention—Cassie's Wolf Den. Could this be Wolf's sister's hair salon? A quick glance at her watch told her she'd missed lunch. Why not take her break at Cassie's? She hurried along the sidewalk. She could use a trim; it had been months since she'd last had one.

Cassie squealed when Becca walked in. "I can't believe you found me! Oh, Becca…," she stepped closer and peered at her bruises, "Wolf told me earlier about your fall and your face. I thought he was exaggerating." Her hands reached to touch and then drew back as if afraid she'd cause pain. "Does it hurt?"

"No. Not like it did last night. You have no idea how much I freaked when I looked in the mirror this morning." *After your brother had ravished me.*

"No doubt. Did Wolf give you my shop's address?"

"No. I was interviewing the owner of Demons and Dolls and saw your sign when I was walking to my car." She glanced around the shop decorated in aquas with splashes of apricot and gold. Next to the cash register stood a fresh tree perfuming the air with pine fragrance. Aqua and gold ornaments and strings of gold beads adorned it. Garlands covered the archway between the reception and hair-care areas. Jazzy Christmas music danced from speakers. A potpourri pot of cinnamon simmered.

"Demons and Dolls? That creep? You interviewed him?"

"Yes. Do you think he's weird, too?" Maybe she'd better do a background check on this guy. He had her reporter radar circling.

Cassie fiddled with a display of hair products. "Slash—don't you just love his name?—is more than weird, if you ask me. Before my grand opening, I visited every tenant in this mall, told them about my business and gave them each a certificate for one free haircut. You know, to build up a relationship. Get some word-of-mouth going." She gave a wave of the hand in emphasis. "Everyone was so nice, except him. I didn't like how he watches the kids who come into his store either."

"You mean he watches to see if they shoplift?" Surely Cassie didn't mean...

"No." The young woman's dark eyes, so like Wolf's, widened. "I mean 'watches.'" She blinked her fingertips in air quotes.

Becca glanced in the direction of the toy store. "I was thinking of checking into the man's background. I'm doing it for sure now."

"Speaking of your job, I hope my brother has gotten over you being a reporter."

A blush warmed her cheeks as she recalled Wolf's calling her name in climax this morning. "Yes, I think we've worked all that out." Could his baby sister see her after-sex glow? "Wow, love your shop. Wolf said he was in yesterday to help you decorate. Do you take walk-ins?"

Cassie fingered Becca's hair. "Wouldn't matter if I did or not. The way my brother keeps talking about you, I'd give you preferential treatment." She pushed her to the stylist area. "What can I do for you? Shampoo and style? Or are we going wild and crazy for the holidays?"

"Wolf is taking me to watch the Holiday Boat Parade from Wendy Anne and Jace's condo." Becca glanced at Cassie. "He said you might be coming."

Cassie opened a black protective cape before laying it over Becca's shoulders and snapping it shut at the back. "If Quinn doesn't forget. I'm not exactly high up on his priority list."

Becca studied her in the mirror. "But you'd like to be?"

The young woman nodded as she combed Becca's hair. "Yeah. I've had a crush on him for a couple years now. The man treats me like his baby sister. How lame is that? The only thing that might work in my favor is the crockpot of Hawaiian meatballs I'm taking. Quinn loves them. Wolf told everyone to bring food so Wendy Anne wouldn't be overwhelmed."

"I thought I'd bring macaroni and cheese and a pan of brownies."

"Sounds fabulous. Jenna's bringing her to-die-for crab dip. Megan has to work late, so she's picking up an order of ready-made tortillas from her favorite Mexican restaurant. I think April said something about a salad. She's watching her weight for her wedding in April."

"April's getting married in April?" Cute. Kinda.

Cassie nodded. "She always said she would." She ran a brush through Becca's hair. "Okay, what are we doing?"

"My hair's almost to my waist. Take about two inches off. Then please can I have a wash and style so I look good for tonight?"

"Will do." Cassie smirked and slipped her cell from her pocket. "Let's rattle big brother's cage, shall we? She thumbed a number and shared an evil conspiratorial grin. "If he yells and barks, he's only marginally upset. Oh, but if he's deathly calm, he is royally pissed. I'll put it on speaker phone."

"Hey, Cassie-Bassie, whatzzup?"

"Need your opinion on something." She leaned against her work counter and winked at Becca.

"Sure."

"Becca's here and—"

"Becca? Let me talk to her." His voice had that soft post-sex quality to it and her hormones sighed in response.

"After you answer our question. See, Becca's thinking about getting a new 'do' for Christmas. Nothing drastic. Just some green streaks to go with her red hair. But here's the thing." She paused and looked at her fingernails—no doubt for effect. "Should she go with dark green like pines for the traditional Christmas colors or a more eye-catching mint green? We need a man's opinion."

Becca covered her mouth with her hands. Oh, Cassie was so good at this. Becca should take lessons from her.

Silence ticked by and Cassie counted off her fingers as she mouthed the numbers, "One…two…three…"

"Put Becca on the phone, please." Something dangerous in the tone of his voice scared her and turned her on at the same time.

Cassie pressed the cell to her chest and stomped her feet a couple times. "Oh, he is soooo damn mad." She leaned side-to-side. "I love it!"

"Cassie, don't play with me. Give. Becca. The phone." Her nipples popped out as if to say they'd talk to him if she wouldn't. Wetness pooled. Why would one angry male turn her on like this? Because it was Wolf, that's why. Oh, she was so screwed where he was concerned.

An effervescent Cassie extended the phone to Becca and she took it. "He…Hello Wolf."

"Sweetheart, you want to tell me what's going on? Why would you want to ruin your beautiful hair?" He sounded so calm, so determined to be in control.

"I felt I needed a change."

"Uh-huh. Why, when you're perfect the way you are?"

"Well, I thought some green highlights would show off the green-lace bra and crotchless panties I just bought."

There was no response.

"Hello…hello?" She looked at Cassie. "We must have been cut off." Her heart sank. "Or he hung up on me."

Cassie's eyes were huge and her mouth gaped open. "Crotchless panties?"

Becca nodded and laughed, handing Cassie her phone.

"Oh, you are so perfect for him. He's such a control freak. It does him good to be knocked off kilter once in a while. I'm betting you'll keep him in line." She slipped her phone into her pocket and folded her arms, her smile sliding from its place of honor. "Wolf also needs to be cared for and pampered. To come first in someone's life. He's never had that. It's he who gives up so much for the family. He was one of the top SEALs and he walked away from the career he loved to take care of us. Me, especially. I was in a really bad place." She rotated her arms to show Becca fine scars on the inside of both forearms. "I'd started cutting myself."

"Oh no." Becca rubbed her fingers over the fine ridges, wincing

78

at the touch.

Cassie nodded. "See, I was so numb from losing Mom and Dad, I couldn't feel anything. I knew I should feel guilt and self-loathing, but hell, I couldn't even cry." She shrugged and tears pooled in her eyes. "So, I started cutting to punish myself."

"You couldn't cry because you were in shock. From what I've read, we all grieve in different ways. I know I grieved after my ex-husband walked out." Becca moved her hand to hold Cassie's. "I was so full of pain and shock, I was numb with it."

"Then you understand." Cassie swiped at a falling tear, and let out a small smile. "Enough of this or you'll have me blubbering like a baby. See, I can cry now." She laughed. "Wolf worked two jobs to pay for my counseling. Now do you see why I adore him? Oh, he makes me mad, but that doesn't change how much I love the big jerk. Come on. Let's get you shampooed."

Cassie talked about her shop and Becca asked her what she was doing especially for Christmas promotion. She might as well include this young entrepreneur in her article about how neighborhood businesses were enticing clients to shop locally.

"I'm going to put on some deep conditioner. You'll have to stay here for five minutes for it to work." Cassie forked fingers through Becca's hair, massaging in the coconut-scented concoction. The shop's phone rang. "Be right back." She hurried off, giving Becca a chance to think.

Had Wolf hung up on her? He'd gone too quiet after she told him about her recent purchase. Did he think she was being too forward? Or was he angry because she'd mentioned crotchless panties in front of his youngest sister? She closed her eyes and sighed. That had to be it. He was so protective of Cassie, of all his sisters. She must have crossed the line. Had he walked out of her life too? After all he'd told her this morning?

Woodsy cologne assailed her nose before warm lips touched hers. Her eyes popped open. Wolf. She moaned and ran her hands over his shoulders. His hands slid under her and lifted her from the chair. Demanding lips slanted and nipped and commanded. Her legs wrapped around his waist and he walked her back against a wall. Just as she teetered before a meltdown, he pulled back and leaned his forehead against hers. "Missed you."

She wiggled against his erection and waggled her eyebrows. "I was about to ask if that was your flashlight or if you were glad to see me."

He leaned in and bit her lower lip. "You drive me crazy. Do you know that? You get me on the phone and taunt me with crotch-less panties. God, woman. I rode the whole way here on my bike sporting a massive woody."

She tilted her head. He was so adorable when he was frustrated with arousal. "Huh…guess we'll have to call your bike a Hard Davidson."

Dark eyes blinked twice at her before Wolf leaned his head back and laughed.

"What are you two doing? Get her head away from my newly painted wall. You'll have conditioner all over it."

He leaned his forehead against hers again. "Busted by a mouthy brat." Becca kept her legs wrapped around his waist as he carried her back to the shampoo station. Once he had her settled on the chair, he kissed her again. He glanced at Cassie. "Did the landlord send an electrician to fix those two outlets?"

She started rinsing Becca's hair. "Nope. Haven't heard a word from him."

"Is his number still in the top drawer?"

"Yes." She turned off the water and squeezed water from Becca's long hair.

"I'll give him a call. Tell him I'll report him to the city if he doesn't get this building up to code. Hell, sparks flew from it when I plugged in my saw the other day." He leaned over and smacked a kiss against Becca's lips. "You ever need a flashlight, sweetheart, you know where to find one."

Indeed, she did.

Chapter 11

Einstein started whining before her doorbell rang.

"What's up with you? Is your buddy out there?" Becca opened the door and the dog charged upstairs. She had a sneaky idea what he was after.

"Hey, beautiful." Wolf stepped inside and enveloped her in his arms. His lips were nearly on hers when a noise upstairs turned his head. "Is that Einstein? What's he doing?"

She exhaled a long-suffering sigh. "Opening my underwear drawer."

He looked at her and then glanced up the steps, the corners of his mouth twitching. "No, seriously, what's he…?"

Her German shepherd proudly galloped down the steps with a pair of pale-blue thongs in his mouth. Wolf started laughing and crouched in front of the dog. His fit of hysterics ratcheted up a couple of notches when Einstein dropped *her* panties onto *his* thigh. She crossed her arms and waited. Finally Wolf wiped his eyes. "Oh, God, I haven't laughed like that in ages. What a helluva dog." He stood and waved the sheer blue thongs. "These are mine, sweetheart. I mean, how can I refuse Einstein's gift?" He shoved them into the pocket of his khakis.

"Both of you are on my shit list." She'd taken special pains with her appearance tonight to impress Wolf. She'd had her hair done and worn her new lingerie. She'd borrowed a Christmas green sweater with a deep u-neckline from Brittany to wear with her good taupe slacks she'd bought on sale last year. Brittany even loaned her a pair of deep-green strappy heels that were a perfect match with the sweater—and, for all her efforts, her dog had taken center stage.

"Hey, come here. Is that a pout?" Wolf ran the pad of his finger over her lips. "I'm thinking the best way to get rid of a pout is to kiss it off." He tugged her close. "You look great, by the way." Then he covered her lips with his and very slowly erased her bad mood.

Kissing Wolf was like having her body massaged in a sauna while someone pumped her hormones full of pleasure juice and drained her mind of all rational thought. The man simply took control of her body. He liquefied her so she sighed into his mouth and melted—simply melted into him.

His hand slid under her hair to cup her neck, and a shiver slithered through every muscle of her body. He backed her against the front door and pressed his thigh between her legs. Wetness pooled in her core. His warm, calloused hand slid under her sweater and feathered up her side to cup her breast, and she moaned. Once again she was astonished at her response to him. It was as if he were the other half to her soul—and didn't *that* just scare the bejesus out of her?

She released his hair, which she'd fisted and slid a hand down over his muscled shoulder to rest against his firm chest. "We're going to be late."

His lips were busy doing marvelous things to her neck. "Don't care." His thumb and fingers were plucking at her nipple, and frankly, she didn't care either.

Einstein nosed between their legs and whined. His paw was on her foot and Wolf shook with laughter. "Your dog is a piece of work."

"I'll let him out for a minute to water the grass and then we better be off."

This was the first time Becca had watched the annual Island Estates Yacht Club's holiday boat parade from the balcony of a second-floor condo, sipping champagne and leaning back against the muscled wall of an ex-SEAL. Normally, she stood along the walkway of Coachman Park alone, even during the times Tommy Ray accompanied her. He was never one for standing closely or showing public displays of affection. Wolf tightened his arms around her waist and leaned his cheek against hers. His woodsy smell did all kinds of things to her feminine system. Evidently, this man had no problems with showing his affection.

She turned her head toward his and he charmed her with a quick kiss. "This is one of my favorite things about living in Clearwater in December."

Wolf nodded. "Yeah, me too. I love seeing the boats decorated with lights and trees and garlands." He glanced at Jace, standing next to them with his hands over Wendy Anne's abdomen, as if protecting their child growing within. "How about we go halves on a boat. Think how I could decorate it next year?"

Jace laughed. "Can't. Got a college fund to sink my extra cash into."

"True that, but don't forget how little junior's aunts and awesomely cool uncle will be contributing to it, too." He pointed toward the causeway. "Wow, look at that one. Red, white and blue lights with a flag all lit up."

Cassie moved next to them, holding hands with Quinn. "I love how the moon shines on the water."

Becca was pleased to see happiness on Cassie's face. She really liked Wolf's youngest sister. "The full moon makes the night magical, doesn't it?"

Wolf turned her slightly and cupped her face, his dark gaze focused solely on her. "You're magical." Then his lips covered hers again.

"Looks like the mighty Wolf has fallen." Quinn leaned an elbow on the railing and grinned.

"Damn straight." The possessive tone of Wolf's reply sent a shiver over her skin. "Looks like the man-whore of Seashell Lane will be burning his little black book."

Becca's head whipped around and met his raised dark eyebrows. *Man-whore? Has he been reading my blog?* She cleared her throat. "Ah…how…how did you find out?"

"The guys at the station are fans of yours. So far they have no clue that the schmuck they've been laughing at is me." He shot a scowl at Quinn. "Of course, once big mouth here blurts it out, I'll be sporting a new nickname at work."

"You? She's been blogging about you all this time?" Quinn beamed a shit-eating grin. "Oh, man, I never put it all together. I just figured she was making this guy up."

Was Wolf angry? He didn't seem angry. In fact, if she didn't know better, she'd guess he enjoyed his anonymous notoriety. Perhaps a man secure in his masculinity could handle the ensuing gentle teasing. "I never used your name."

He kissed her nose. "No, but how many women-magnets do you know?" He winked and then hugged her. "I'm warning you, our love life is not fodder for your blog. I'm drawing the line at that."

She bit his square jaw. "Yes, Wolf…" A low chuckle rumbled from her chest.

"Becca. I mean it…"

"Oh, look at that one." Wendy Anne pointed. Applause and cheers proclaimed the spectators' approval of a boat decorated completely with blue lights except for a golden star at the top of the mast. Strains of "Silent Night" floated across the water toward all the spectators. Applause and cheers proclaimed their approval.

Megan, still in her scrubs, reclined on a lounge at the side of the balcony. "You're right. That boat's lovely. But that red and white boat behind looks like a giant floating candy cane. How pretty." She palmed a yawn. "Would someone bring me a cup of coffee and one of Becca's brownies? I'm too tired to stand. Twelve hours of running up and down hospital corridors plays havoc on my legs."

Wolf pulled away from Becca. "I'll get it. Do you want anything, Becca?"

"No, I'm good."

He leaned in and kissed her again. "You sure as hell are." His lips teased hers when he spoke. "As soon as the last boat passes, I'm taking you home."

A jolt of desire sparked her synapses and all points south. Yay for me!

They decided on the way home to sleep at Becca's. Einstein would need a short walk and Wolf had to be at the station early in the morning. While he grabbed a change of clothes and his toothbrush, she took her dog for his late-night stroll. She was brushing him down when Wolf strode in, carrying an overnight bag.

He set it in the hallway and watched her, smiling. "You take good care of him."

"This is part of our nightly ritual. I walk him, brush his coat to calm him down and then send him to his chair with a chew toy." She put the brush in a drawer and handed Einstein a piece of beef-flavored rawhide. "Go get in your chair now." She snapped her fingers and her pet obeyed.

She filled the coffeepot with water. "What time do you want the coffee to start brewing? I'll set the timer on the maker."

"Five."

"That's ungodly. I don't see how you do it." She opened the cabinet and pulled out the bean-grinder. "As soon as I get the coffee set, I'll be ready to go upstairs."

Wolf stepped behind her, the heat of his nearness a comforting presence. "Are you planning to spoil me, too?" He pushed her hair off her neck and planted three kisses below her hairline.

Her body reacted and a shiver woke her nipples for playtime. "If…if you don't stop that, I'll lose count of how many scoops of coffee beans I've got in the grinder."

His deep laughter of male enjoyment brought on a smile. The

man had a way about him.

"I'll take my stuff upstairs."

Once she had the timer set, she turned out the lights and kissed Einstein good night before going upstairs. When she stepped into her room, the glow of candlelight welcomed her. The sheets were turned back and red rose petals were scattered across the bed. Soft guitar music played. She turned and Wolf stood in the doorway to the master bath, his muscles gleaming in the shine and shadows of the flickering candles.

"You set a romantic scene, Dan Wolford."

He stalked toward her, wearing nothing but black boxers. "I went shopping for a few things after leaving Cassie's shop earlier. He held a hand behind him. "I bought the candles and rose petals." He moved his hand. His long fingers curled around a small box. "And this." He placed the box in her palm.

"What have you done?"

"I'm a proprietary person. Don't like anyone riding my Harley or using my diving equipment." He snapped open the jeweler's box. "And I don't want anyone getting ideas about you. If you chose to break off things between us, that's one thing, but I can guarantee you it won't be me."

She removed a diamond heart on a silver chain from the box. "This is too much. We only met a few weeks ago."

He knew how to rattle her soul, to shake the folds out so it was no longer compacted but unfurling, like a flag in the wind.

"I thought I made it clear this morning how I feel about you. We didn't just have sex, we mated." He tucked two fingers under her chin. "I don't know about you, but I've fallen in love."

"Every man I've ever loved has left me." Twin tears found their way onto her cheeks, their moisture scalding.

"Maybe they weren't man enough to complete the mission." He slipped the chain from her fingers and stepped behind her. "Lift your hair, sweetheart." The coolness of silver kissed her skin. Wolf's palms rubbed down her arms, sending sensations of belonging to this man to saturate every cell in her body. When he reached her hands, he intertwined his fingers with hers. "Now, when someone asks you whose heart you have, tell them you have mine."

She turned into his arms. "I love it, Wolf. It's beautiful." She kissed him. "Everything seems so right between us. It's almost scary."

His strong arms tightened around her, bringing her closer. "Tell me. Tell me you're mine." He kissed her again, his lips taking command while her heart whispered yes. Kisses were feathered across her cheeks. Teeth nipped her neck and his tongue soothed. A hand cupped her derriere and squeezed. "Now, about these crotchless panties you're wearing..."

Chapter 12

Becca settled into her usual chair for the editor's regular morning meeting. Making love to Wolf several times during the night and again early this morning had her a little sore, but it was the kind of discomfort that made her smile. He'd left her a note by the coffeemaker: "Loved sleeping next to you. Took the 'thong thief' for a walk. Check out your front yard." When she'd hurried to her bay window, Wolf's inflatable bear holding a heart was in her yard facing her window. The man knew how to charm her, that was for sure.

Her fingers fluttered to the diamond heart he'd given her last night and she recalled the promise she'd made to him—she was his. Now, if only he remained hers and didn't eventually walk out of her life too.

"How's your holiday shopping piece coming along, Becca?" Marshall's unibrow furrowed like a caterpillar in movement.

"I'll have it to you within the hour. I think you'll be pleased."

"Good." He turned to the sports editor. "How'd your interview with the manager of the Buccaneers go? What did he have to say about free agency this year?"

Becca tuned out the conversation and worked on how she would approach Marshall about her idea. He wasn't always the easiest man to get around, but she'd done some initial research on Slash and didn't like what she'd learned. She smelled a good story.

Marshall clapped his hands once, his traditional signal the meeting was over. It was now or never. She raised her hand.

"Yes, Becca?"

"I've turned up some things on initial research and I'd like your permission to dig deeper."

"Into…?" His unibrow was on the move again.

"Slash Harper, the owner of Demons and Dolls Toy Store. I interviewed him yesterday and something pricked my radar."

Her editor made a rolling motion with his hand to signal her to hurry up. The man had no patience.

"He's been charged twice with child molestation. Once in Boston and again in Atlanta. He shouldn't be anywhere near children, yet he's got a toy store."

"Did he serve any time?"

"No. But to be charged twice…" She leaned forward and held up two fingers.

"Okay. Do a full background check. Bring your research to me and we'll talk. I'll have to inform the police too." Marshall ran a hand across the back of his neck. "What's he doing running a toy store? Hell, my grandson goes there."

Two hours later, Becca entered Demons and Dolls. She needed a picture of Slash. In the ones she'd found online, he had shaggy hair. But now his head was shaved with a tattoo of a slash down the side of his bald scalp and he wore glasses. Court records showed his real name was Marvin Harper. She had to be sure she had the right guy.

Slash looked up from a box he was unpacking. "Back so soon?"

"Yeah. I need one of your wolf figurines." She'd give it to Wolf for Christmas.

"Second aisle, about halfway on your left." He was examining a doll, looking under its skirt. Her skin crawled. Ew. Creepy.

She picked a figurine she thought Wolf might like and carried it to the register. "My editor wants some pictures for the article I interviewed you for yesterday." She slipped her camera from her pants pocket. "Mind if I snap a couple of shots of your store?"

"Sure. As long as I'm not in any of 'em."

She made a show of snapping several pictures of a display of French porcelain dolls and a shelf of demon warriors, getting closer to him with every shot she took. As soon as she got his complete face at the edge of a frame, she snapped several in rapid-fire succession. He scowled. "Don't worry. I think I only got your shoulder, but I can crop it out. I'll probably zoom in some so I can get that unusual collection of dollhouse furniture over your shoulder."

"See that you do. That'll be thirty-two fifty for the wolf."

Handing him her charge card, she propped an elbow on his glass counter. "Is that a Boston accent I detect? My Uncle Ben lives just outside of Boston. He's been there since he got out of high school."

Slash narrowed his eyes and handed back her card. "Sign here." He slid the charge slip toward her. Evidently, he wasn't going to answer her question. He placed her item in a bag and slapped it on the counter. "I think we're done." His eyes were hard and cold. A shiver of danger danced up her spine.

The sirens of approaching fire trucks snagged her attention and she hurried outside. Two rolled into the parking lot of the strip mall and stopped in front of Cassie's beauty shop. Becca took off running. Smoke rolled out of the building. Oh no, this couldn't be happening. Where was Cassie?

She found her leaning against her silver compact car, crying.

"Hey." Becca opened her arms and Cassie stepped into them for a hug. "What happened?"

"I don't know. I was mixing dye for a customer and the sprinklers went off. I called nine-one-one right away. Smoke started rolling out." Cassie sobbed against her blouse. "My dream is going up in smoke. The whole family, Wolf especially, worked so hard to get it the way I wanted it." She pulled back and wiped tears from her moistened cheeks.

Another fire truck rumbled in, its siren piercing her ears.

Cassie glanced at the arriving apparatus. "Wolf and Jace's fire crew is here. I knew they'd come."

Becca wrapped her arm around Cassie's shoulders.

Once the fire truck screeched to a halt, its diesel engine rumbling, Jace jumped off and ran toward them, his rubber boots clunking on the pavement. "Cassie, you okay? Need medical treatment, honey?"

"No, I'm fine. Honest."

Jace nodded at Becca. More sirens sounded, and he glanced over his shoulder. "That's our ladder truck. Wolf and Quinn are coming on it. Gotta go. Call Wendy Anne, tell her you're okay. She'll have heard on Twitter or Facebook and be worried." He dashed to retrieve equipment off the rig.

Cassie tugged her phone from her pocket and thumbed a text. "Be easier to text the whole family at once. Tell them what's happened and that Wolf and Jace are here."

"Do you mind if I take some pictures for the paper? I might as well report on it." She could download them to her laptop in her car, write up a quick article and e-mail it to Marshall.

"Hey, go ahead. Might need copies for insurance purposes." Cassie's thumbs were clacking on the mini-keyboard. She stopped and burst into tears again. "My…my beautiful shop. It's gone."

Becca enveloped her into her arms once more. "You'll have another one. You've got insurance, right?" Cassie nodded. "I'll see you get copies of my pictures. You'll have a place of business again. I'm sure of it." She dug in her purse and handed Cassie a tissue.

"Thanks. I'll be fine now. I think that last bit of crying did it for me. Time to get mad and get even, as Wolf says. Go on. Take your pictures." She waved her off.

"I'll call my editor so he doesn't send out someone else. Are you sure you'll be okay alone here for a couple minutes while I get my car from the other end of the mall?"

"I'm good. As good as I can be, with my livelihood reduced to ashes."

Becca stepped along the front of the building and snapped pictures. Something called to her, searing her. When she lowered the camera, Wolf had stopped halfway on the extending ladder, his protective gear blocking most of his face. Even so, anger vibrated off him so palpably it speared its way into her being.

She raised a hand to wave, but he returned his attention to the job at hand, climbing and hoisting the hose farther up the aerial ladder. He couldn't be upset with her, not after the magical night they'd shared and all the things he'd told her. No doubt he was worried about Cassie and she had just picked up on his anxiety.

Her phone to her ear, she hurried to her car, waiting for Marshall to answer her call.

"Yeah."

"Just calling to tell you I'm at the scene of a fire at the Goodwinds Strip Mall on Pinella. I'll take pictures and write up a short article. No need to send someone else out. I'll e-mail everything to you."

"Sounds good. Did you get a picture of Slash?"

"Yeah. I asked if I could take shots of the interior of his store. He said not to take any of him, but I got two pictures at least."

"Good girl. You're going to make a first-rate reporter yet."

She disconnected the call, felt the hair on the back of her neck stand straight out and turned to stare into the pinched face of Slash Harper.

His hand coiled around her neck and he slammed her against her car. "You meddling bitch. Didn't I tell you not to take pictures of me?"

She shook her head. "I...I didn't."

He snatched her cell from her and flung it across the parking lot. "Good at lyin', aren't ya? I had a good thing goin' here until you stuck your nose in." He squeezed her throat tighter. "Guess who paid me a visit as soon as you walked out? The police." His head jerked in the direction of Cassie's shop. "They left to check out that fire, but not before asking me some questions about my

92

priors." He thumped her head against the roof of her car.

Fear wrapped its icy fingers around her lungs and tightened. She couldn't breathe. Couldn't swallow. Black spots danced in front of her eyes. She had to get away. Her eyes darted toward the roof of the mall, where Wolf worked to put out the flames. Who would help her?

Slash leaned against her, his putrid breath making her gag. "Everyone's attention is on the fire. No one's watching what's going on here." His other hand clutched her breast. "Bet I could take you right here against the car and no one would notice. 'Course my tastes run to the younger stuff. But a revenge fuck can be good, too."

Dear God, help me. Wolf, I need you.

Chapter 13

Wolf seethed with anger as he worked to contain the fire. When he'd arrived on the scene, Becca was already there, interviewing Cassie. His heart twisted when he saw his baby sister crying and his resentment toward all reporters galled. Hadn't Cassie been through enough at the hands of the news-hungry media?

He'd thought Becca above all that. In fact, he'd rationalized her presence by thinking she was just offering support. Then she started taking pictures of the burning building, no doubt for her newspaper. What a fool he'd been to believe in her. She was no better than any other damn reporter.

A warning, a plea filtered into his consciousness. Help me, Wolf...I need you. He raised his head and zeroed in on Becca at her car with a man standing over her. Damn, from here it looked as if he had his hands on her. Wolf blinked. Wolf, help me! My God, he was choking her!

Wolf depressed a button and spoke into his mouthpiece. "Tell the cops there's a woman being accosted at her beige car at the opposite end of the mall."

"You sure, man?"

"Yeah. It's a reporter I used to date. Tell them to hurry."

For all his annoyance and disappointment toward Becca, he didn't want her hurt. Every instinct screamed at him to go to her. Protect her. Kill the sonofabitch who dared put his hands on the woman he loved—loved and yet disliked. He turned back to battle the blaze, scrambling over the roof to reach another potential hotspot. He had a job to do. No matter how much the man in him wanted to protect Becca, the fireman in him had to extinguish the fire. This was how he earned his livelihood. People depended on him.

Wasn't being a reporter how Becca earned her income?

Hell, she didn't have to question Cassie while her dream burned.

But, what of Becca's dream? Didn't she have a right to do what she loved, too?

God, he hated being the ass. Of course she had a right to do whatever she desired. He cared for her, the warm woman who liked to grumble and tease. She completed him. He couldn't describe how or why. He just knew she was the woman for him. Reporter or not, she completed his soul.

He glanced over his shoulder. A policeman was talking to Becca. The asshole who'd touched her lay sprawled on the ground with another officer's knee in his back. Wolf breathed a sigh of relief and returned to his task. The woman he loved was okay.

****

"Miss Sinclair, I've arranged for an ambulance to take you to the hospital. It's procedure to have victims of sexual assault examined. A trained counselor will speak with you."

She focused on the kind officer, trembling more as each second passed. "I…I don't want to go to the hospital. I wasn't…" she clutched her torn top to her breasts and her teeth chattered, "…I…I wasn't raped. Just groped and scared shitless. If you hadn't come when you did, I might not have been so lucky."

"You can thank your ex-boyfriend for that." He jerked a thumb over his shoulder.

"Ex…ex-boyfriend?" Surely the officer had misunderstood.

He glanced from the notes he scribbled in a notebook. "Yeah, Dan Wolford. 'Course we just call him Wolf. He saw the man attacking you and called it in. Said you were a reporter he used to date."

Her shaking increased. "U…used to…" Tinkling sounds filtered through her mind as her heart shattered into tiny shards. *I'm a reporter he used to date.*

"Too bad you two couldn't make a go of it. He's a helluva nice guy. Sure does take care of his family."

Wolf must have seen her talking to Cassie when the ladder truck arrived. Had he thought she was interviewing his sister during her crisis? She groaned. Cassie was crying, so, of course, he assumed she was asking his sister questions, not offering support. Her shoulders slumped. Did he think so little of her?

Now that her examination was over and the upsetting interview with the sexual-abuse crisis counselor finished, Becca waited for Brittany to come and take her home. The doctor had prescribed something for her headache. Her poor old noggin had taken a beating these last few days. First, the box of shelves fell on it and then Slash had pounded it repeatedly against the roof of her car. Still, for all that, her head had fared better than her heart.

They were so early into their relationship and already Wolf had walked out of her life—without a proper good-bye or an attempt at explaining. She'd been a fool to let him into her life and her bed. What was wrong with her? Why did every man eventually walk away from her? Scalding tears burned paths down her cheeks, and Becca retreated inside her battered and broken soul.

A cool hand to her cheek jarred her from her internal painful place. "Britt." Her mouth was so dry. "I need a drink."

"So do I, girlfriend, after seeing your face." Brittany handed her a cup of iced water. "Does it hurt?"

The cool liquid soothed her damaged windpipe. "Every part of me hurts," she rasped. "Being strangled is no fun. Doc says I'll talk like this for a few days."

"You sure you're fit to go home? I can stay the night."

"Not needed. I'd sooner be alone. Just get me out of this place. I'll explain everything in the car." She opened her arms. "I need a hug, Britt." In the moments that followed, she realized how much she could still cry. Was there no end to the tears?

It was nearly eight when Brittany eased her clunker to the curb in front of Becca's. Her blue eyes narrowed and swept to Wolf's townhouse. "His lights are on. I ought to go over there and smack him."

"He's at the station, working two twenty-four-hour shifts. I think he has his lights on timers."

"I've heard a lot of stupid reasons for dumping someone, but to drop you because you're a reporter is some sick shit."

Becca smiled and reached out to take Brittany's hand. "Double-B's." They'd called themselves that since their junior year in high school.

"Better and Best." Brittany squeezed her hand. "Love you."

"Love you, too. Come inside. Or better still, take Einstein for a walk. I'm taking a hot bath and going to bed."

"I'll make you tomato soup and a grilled cheese."

"You know me so well. Come on."

Einstein was all over her when she stepped inside. He sniffed her from head to toe, whining and licking. "Did Baby miss Mommy?" She planted a kiss on the top of his head and he slurped her right back. "What would I do without you?"

Brittany pulled his leash from the coat closet doorknob. "Want to go for a walk, Einstein?" She pointed to Becca. "You go take a bath."

Becca stood at the doorway to her bedroom. The room she'd shared with Wolf last night. Rose petals littered the floor and her linens. Her purple sheets were still a tangled mess from their early-morning lovemaking. She shook her head once. No, not love. Sex. Love would involve some trust. If Wolf truly loved her, he'd have known she would never cause Cassie any harm or discomfort.

She rushed to her bed and yanked off the sheets and blankets. At the top of the steps, she heaved them downward and then stomped down the steps to kick them to the bottom of the stairway. Because it felt so damn good, she kicked them down the hallway to the laundry closet in her kitchen.

"Damn him. Damn him for making me fall in love. For making me feel again. And for making me hurt inside like I've never hurt before." She shoved two blankets into the washer and added soap and softener. Once the machine had started, she leaned over it, hugged the appliance and bawled as she cursed the world and one particular man living in it.

Her tantrum over, she straightened and went upstairs. She tugged her favorite pansy-flowered sheets from the linen closet and made up her bed. Then she scooped the dried rose petals from her floor and dumped them into her trashcan, along with the burnt candles. Anything that reminded her of Wolf went into the can—the strand of pearls, her feather pen and condom wrappers. She carried it outside to the dumpster, along with the arrangement of flowers he'd gotten her.

When she returned, her attention snagged on the inflatable bear in her yard. With great glee, she strode over toward the bear, kicked it down and stomped on it.

"What in H-E-double toothpicks are you doing now?"

Becca clapped her hand over her heart. "Mrs. Minelli, you scared me."

Her elderly neighbor marched to Becca's side. "Romance is over, huh? Bad in the sack was he? Let me guess, he was built like a moose and hung like a mouse."

"No. Not at all, and that's all I'm sharing of my sex life. He hurt me." She jumped on the bear decoration again and took a perverse pleasure when it popped. "This is how he stomped on my heart."

"Just what the world needs. Another drama queen. Maybe you ought to give up men for Bingo and water aerobics."

Becca snatched the destroyed decoration from her yard and tossed it onto Wolf's front porch. "That might not be a bad idea."

"Darlin', take a bit of advice from a senior citizen. People are gonna hurt you. It's a fact of life. What you have to ask yourself is which weighs more on the scales of life? What he brings to your heart or the occasional time he mucks things up and hurts you. After all, you're not perfect either. None of us are, but most of us are worthy of love." She patted Becca's arm and turned toward her townhouse. "Gotta get home to George before his Viagra pill wears off."

Once inside her home, she tossed her washed blankets into the dryer and pushed her sheets, smelling of roses, Wolf and sex into the washer.

All physical traces of Wolf gone, she ran back upstairs and started her bath. She passed the mirror and stilled. Her diamond heart blinked and teased in the mirror's reflection. His gift to her. Evidently, the necklace was more valuable than his promises.

Her front door opened. "Becca, we're back. Are you still awake?"

"Yes. Just about to get in the tub. I had to put clean sheets on the bed."

Einstein propped his nose on the edge of the tub as she bathed. The hot water soothed her aching muscles, clearing some of the mental fog from her thinking processes. She had to admit she shouldered some of the blame for her broken heart. Hadn't she guarded it this past year? Yet, as soon as one dark-eyed man with a lone dimple aimed a smile her way, she lowered her guard. "Stupid, stupid, stupid."

Her dog whined and rested a paw on the tub. She leaned toward him and he licked her face.

"Looks like it's just you and me from now on. And no more carrying my underwear next door to that man. You hear?"

He barked twice.

"Don't you talk back to me." She stood and dried off. "Do I need to rearrange my drawers?"

He growled deep in his throat, turned and sat with his back toward her. And wasn't that just like a man?

Chapter 14

Becca fumbled in her sleep to answer the phone. The sunlight glaring in her windows made her wince, and she covered her face with a pillow. "Hello?"

"Why in hell won't you answer your cell or return my texts?"

At the sound of Wolf's voice, a lump of pain formed in her chest. She opened and closed her mouth twice, willing her vocal chords to work.

"I've been out of my damn mind with worry. I called the hospital, but they said you were released last night."

"Why? Why do you care what happened to me?"

"You can ask me that?" His voice had that deadly quiet about it. The man was angry and she didn't give a damn. "What's wrong with your voice?"

"I've had damage to my windpipe." *And to my sense of security and to my love-damaged heart.*

"Jesus, did that man choke you?"

"Oh, and like you really care! Don't pretend something you don't feel. Look, I'm sorry you couldn't reach me. Slash, the man who attacked me, threw my phone away. Besides, why would you want to call a 'reporter you used to date'? I believe those were your exact words when you described me to the police."

Wolf cursed into the phone.

"Don't call me again. You lied to me, and I was dumb enough to believe you. You'll never get beyond the fact I'm a reporter, and I'll never trust you won't turn your back on me again." She ended the call and crawled out of bed. If she hurried, she could grab a cup of coffee and a donut on her way to work.

Marshall approached her desk. "Wasn't expecting you in today."

"I have a job to do. News needs reporting." Wolf's remarks about the lack of sincerity in reporters came back to her, and she pushed them aside.

Marshall's unibrow shifted. "You up to doing the piece on your attack?"

She nodded. "I'm working on it now." Actually, it was helping her deal with the trauma to write about it.

"E-mail the article to me when you're done. I'm leading with it today." Her boss turned to leave and she grabbed this opportunity. "Marshall? The firemen in the city are doing their annual toy ride day after tomorrow. I'll be one of the participants. Want me to take some pictures and interview a few people? Might make a good human-interest piece."

He nodded. "Might."

"It's their twentieth year doing this."

A slow smile creased his wrinkled face. "You're still after that column, aren't you?"

She crossed her arms. "I've got fourteen hundred and twelve followers. Worldwide."

"Yes, and my wife is one of them. She reads your blog to me every morning over breakfast." He shook his head. "That damn Bull. I laugh like a loon every time you write about him. He must be the biggest dumbass in the whole state."

"Oh, Boss, you got that right."

****

Wolf was in one hellish dark mood. Not only had he doubted

102

Becca, but thanks to his big mouth, she knew about it. He'd hurt her, which was something he'd promised her he'd never do. Now he'd have to fight like hell, possessed to win her back. What made things extra difficult was his work schedule. He was tied to this station for another twenty-one hours. Every job had its drawbacks.

Like having to interview people at their most painful times.

Wolf cursed and changed rags to rub over the chrome of fire truck number two. If there was one thing that pained a man more than heartburn or kidney stones or hemorrhoids, it was his conscience bugging the hell out of him when he was wrong.

"Got a minute?" Jace stood in front of him. He'd been so lost in thought, he hadn't heard or seen his brother approach.

He spared him a grunt and kept on polishing the chrome.

"How are things between you and Becca?" Jace leaned against the truck.

Acid rolled. He was not in the mood for this. "Piss-poor, if you must know."

"Is that why you aren't talking to anyone?" Jace glanced over his shoulder. "Fellas think you're mad at them for something. They're in there organizing the toys that've been donated so far and you're out here wiping phantom dust off apparatus."

"I'm not in the mood for polite chitchat." He tossed the rag aside and slipped his hands in his pockets.

"Not even with your own brother?" Jace's eyebrows rose. "Oh, that's right. Your *younger* brother. Hell, you won't confide in me. Never have. Not about the important stuff."

He scowled at Jace. The big brother wasn't supposed to confide. He was supposed to listen, act and do whatever it took to solve family problems.

"You're so hung up on being *the* big brother and doing for us that you forget maybe we'd like to help you through life, too." Jace sighed, as if reading Wolf's mind. "We're brothers, man. I should be able to offer you advice or protect your back, but you're too damn stubborn to lean on anyone." Jace lifted his hands and let them fall. "Hell, no wonder you're having problems with Becca if you won't lean on her."

"Me lean on her? Hell, a man's job is to protect his woman. I couldn't even do that when she was being attacked." His male pride had taken a huge beating over that. Being tied to his job when the woman he loved needed him had made him feel powerless. And he was damned mad over it all.

"Man, you need to get over some of this sexist shit."

"Sexist? I'm the least sexist—"

"Women are hellishly strong. Sure, we're supposed to look out for them, but we have to lean on them too. Look, any human who can squeeze into a dress and skimpy panty hose and those damn high stilettos to dance *backwards* is no weakling."

Sometimes his little brother knew how to bean him between the eyes. The corners of his mouth twitched. "Man, that's some deep shit."

"Honest to God, Wolf, it's like I told Wendy Anne. I look at you sometimes and see the hamster wheel turning, but the hamster's dead."

Wolf slapped a hand over his eyes and sighed. Where the hell did the kid get his logic? Still, he had to admit Jace was able to keep his wife happy; something he hadn't been able to do with Becca. Maybe he could learn a thing or two from him after all. He clasped a hand on his brother's shoulder. "How about a soda and a long talk?"

****

The following afternoon, Becca stopped partway on her outside steps. A live four-foot Christmas tree in a pot stood next to her front door. It was decorated with purple and lavender bulbs. An angel graced the top. Wide iridescent silver ribbon twisted and wrapped around the small branches. A card was nestled within the pine.

She opened the envelope and tugged on the card. An empty doghouse was on the front with the words, "The only thing missing is me." She sighed, struggling between the urge to open it or tear it up. *Whatever Wolf wrote will only bring me pain. I can't deal with this right now, not after all I dreamed last night.*

During the night she'd felt Slash's hands on her throat and woken up screaming. Einstein had barreled up the steps, barking. He'd needed comforting almost as much as she had once she realized she was safe at home. Although she'd never allowed her dog to sleep with her, last night she did. Bless his heart, he'd kept the nightmares away.

After work, when she approached her car, she'd had another bad episode. If one of her male coworkers hadn't walked up behind her, startling her, she would have been okay. But he had—and she'd freaked. The man merely wanted to compliment her on her article about the child predator operating a toy store, but the poor guy barely knew how to handle her hysterics.

She'd scrambled into her car, locked the doors and trembled for ten minutes before she found her center and regained composure.

Now she stood in front of a let's-make-up present from Wolf. No, she couldn't read his card. Maybe in a few days. Not today. Einstein barked and whined. "Shush, now. Mommy will be in soon. Go get in your chair and lay down."

So, what would she do with the tree? Take it inside or leave it out on her porch? Her cell rang and she fished it out of her purse. Wolf. She wouldn't answer. No, that would be childish.

"Hello."

"You got a new phone." She could almost hear the smile in his voice.

"Yes." She wouldn't give in to him.

"Are you home, sweetheart?" His voice all but purred over the phone.

The jerk. "Yes, and I'm staring at a Christmas tree. Why did you send it? I told you things were over between us." There, she'd said it. His smiles and his sexy voice hadn't gotten to her.

"Did you read the card?"

"No. I can't…" she rubbed a hand over her eyes, surprised to find them damp with tears, "it's been a rough day." Her voice cracked and she winced.

"Will you tell me about it tomorrow on the toy ride?"

Her stomach twisted with nerves. "No. I'm riding alone."

"I don't think so. You've had a physically rough week. Baby, I have to go. Promise me you'll read the note." He ended the call.

She sat on her steps, tapping the card on her knee. A neighbor across the street waved, and she raised her hand in greeting. Two boys rode their skateboards down the pavement. A lady jogged by with her dog. Becca rubbed her thumb over the edge of the card. *If I read this, I'll break. I'll crack in half and then fracture into pain-filled pieces.* She slid the card into her back pocket and checked for messages on her phone. She played a video game on her screen.

Oh, what the hell. She opened the card and ignored the printed message, going straight for Wolf's words. My God, he'd written a poem.

If I came to you on a starlit night,

Would you allow me to make things right?

Would my love grant me the wishes

Of your eternal love and sweet kisses,

And your promise to be mine—forever?

She folded her arms on her knees, laid her forehead down on them and sobbed. How could he keep doing this to her?

"Don't cry, baby." Wolf scooped her into his arms and sat in her place. His warmth was a sweet balm to her battered soul.

Becca swiped tears from her face, surprised to see him. "Why aren't you at work?"

"I took some personal time." His hand cupped her cheek. "I had to see you. Needed to see you. I'm sorry for the way I reacted when I saw you talking to Cassie at the fire."

"I was *talking* to her, not interviewing her."

His arms tightened and his brown eyes studied her face. "Even if you had been interviewing her, you have a right to do your job."

She pressed her hand over his mouth. "Wait a minute. Repeat that." Surely she hadn't heard him correctly.

"You're a reporter. I have to trust you'll show some humanity in your job. I think I'm familiar enough with your principles to know you will. That's why I was so wrong to get furious with you." He sighed and tipped his forehead against hers. "I broke a promise and emotionally walked away."

"Am I hearing this right? You're okay with my being a reporter?"

His fingers trailed down her cheek. "I don't care what you are as long as you're mine. My obsessive dislike of reporters was wrong."

This was the last thing she had expected, yet the one thing she needed. "Our problems boil down to trust, don't they? Your trust of me as a reporter and my trusting you to stay with me for the long haul."

He played with her fingers and then lifted his gaze to hers. "When I turned my back on you at the fire, all I did was reinforce your fears."

She shook her head and swiped away tears. "I should have trusted you."

"I need you in my life. Once we both accept that, everything else is minor." He covered her lips with his and a jolt of electric flash burned through her system. She wrapped her arms around his broad shoulders and inhaled his woodsy cologne. Everything about him drew her like a magnet. Lips rubbed and teased. Tongues met and dueled. Sighs and moans mingled.

The tapping of a cane grew closer, and Wolf's shoulders shook

107

with laughter.

"What in H-E-double toothpicks are you two doing now? If you're going to have make-up sex, take it inside. By golly, I thought my George was frisky, but, Wolf, I think you've got him beat." Mrs. Minelli shook her cane at him. A wide, denture-filled smile spread. "I'm glad you two made up. Carry on." She turned and teetered off before glancing back over her shoulder. "Just take it inside."

Becca stood and smiled. Make-up sex with Wolf ought to be phenomenal. "Einstein needs a walk first."

As if he got her meaning, he stood and smiled too. "You take him. I'll carry in the tree."

"Deal." She unlocked the door and gasped.

"What?" Wolf glanced over her shoulder and started laughing.

Einstein sat in the middle of a pile of thongs and bras, a red lace bra hanging from his mouth.

The twentieth annual Fireman's Toy Run was slated to start at nine at Station Thirty-two—ten minutes from now. The sky was blue and temperatures warm. It promised to be a beautiful day for a ride. Every make and modification of motorcycle was lined up. Quinn was busy handing out numbers to participants. Elvis' "Blue Christmas" blared from the speakers. Spirits were high.

"What the hell am I going to do?" Wolf threw up his hands, his backside hanging out of the moth-eaten suit.

Becca couldn't stop laughing. The look on Wolf's face when he had bent over and the suit ripped was priceless. She glanced at the clock. "We don't have much time. You have to do something."

He pulled her close and kissed her for the zillionth time that day. It was as if he couldn't get enough of her. "What do you suggest?"

"Put on your leather pants. You wore them here. Wear the Santa shirt and beard. You'll look great." They didn't have much choice in the matter if the ride was to start on time.

"That'll work." Wolf unbuttoned the fly of the old red-wool pants. His head rose and he shot her an embarrassed expression.

"Ah…this isn't going into your article, is it? The part about me ripping the ass out of the Santa suit?"

She folded her arms over her elf suit. "No. Why would you ask?"

"Becca…"

She buffed her nails on her pink and purple-striped top and stared at them for a beat. "Okay, so there might be a mention in the paper tomorrow that Santa wore leathers." On impulse, she made a fist and held it lengthwise in front of his mouth as if it were a microphone. "So tell me, Santa, how did it feel to buck tradition by changing wool for leathers?"

Wolf grabbed her upper arms and hauled her to him. "Not nearly as good as it's going to feel to make love to one of my elves over the handlebars of my Harley."

She batted her eyes. "Ohhhh, Santa."